P9-CEZ-052

Also by Joan Lowery Nixon:

The Dark and Deadly Pool
The Ghosts of Now
The Other Side of Dark
Secret, Silent Screams
The Specter
The Stalker

Whispers from the Dead

Whispers from the Dead

by Joan Lowery Nixon

Delacorte Press

Published by Delacorte Press
Bantam Doubleday Dell Publishing Group, Inc.
666 Fifth Avenue, New York, New York 10103

Library of Congress Cataloging in Publication Data
Nixon, Joan Lowery.
    Whispers from the dead / Joan Lowery Nixon.
    p.   cm.
    Summary: After making contact with the spirit world
during a near-death experience, Sara moves
to Houston with her parents and receives otherworldly
messages about a murder committed in her house.
    ISBN 0-385-29809-9
    [1. Supernatural—Fiction. 2. Murder—Fiction.
3. Mystery and detective stories.]   I. Title.
PZ7.N65Wh   1989   [Fic]—dc19
89-1555   CIP   AC

Book design by Andrew Roberts

Manufactured in the United States of America
October 1989
10 9 8 7 6 5 4 3 2 1

BG

For my aunt
Genevieve Meyer
with love

Whispers from the Dead

Prologue

Because the things that happened to me were so strange, I know that some people will find them hard to believe. It's like when your mind slides from sleeping to waking and something takes place that's so bizarre, you tell yourself, "I have to be dreaming. This couldn't be real." Or when you jolt awake from a nightmare, and there are still unfamiliar shapes that move through your dark room, and you stare at them with wide-open eyes, knowing they can't exist and you must be awake.

There will be more questions, and I'll have to repeat the answers over and over—even to myself—so I've bought a thick, yellow, lined tablet, and I'm going to write down everything that took place, beginning with the day I died.

■

My name is Sarah Darnell. I'm sixteen—almost seventeen—and I'm tall, with long, curly, dark hair. I'm a little bit underweight, but—

No. That's not the way to start this story, with facts like those on a driver's license. I'll have to start at the beginning, when we lived in Springdale, Missouri, before we moved to Houston, and write about the drowning. I hate to write about it because I know the cold and the terror will crawl back into my mind and I won't be able to hide from it, but I haven't got a choice. You'll have to know what happened.

It was a Saturday morning, and Marcie, my best friend, had telephoned early, waking me. "Andy just called," she said. "Everybody's going to the lake. Come on. Get out of bed and grab your bathing suit. We'll pick you up in half an hour."

Summer had come early this year, spring flowers barely budding before wilting in the heat, but I pulled the sheet up over my head and shivered. "The water will still be cold," I complained.

Marcie laughed, and I could picture her wide, lopsided smile. "Not that cold," she said. "Come on. Andy and Barbie are bringing some stuff so we can cook hot dogs, and Kent's mom just made a batch of cookies. It's going to be fun."

It would be. All of us had been good friends since we

were little kids, and I didn't want to be left out of the party. "I'll be ready," I said.

I was right about the water, so cold that it made us gasp for breath and yell and thrash around until we got used to it and raced each other out to the old float. Andy got there first. He grabbed my hand and helped me scramble up the side of the float. "You're looking good," he said, not letting go of my hand. "I like that bathing suit."

I grinned at him. I'd had a big crush on Andy a few years ago and tagged after him whenever I could—a lovesick seventh-grader impressed by a boy two years older, taller than I was, and strong enough to smash soft-drink cans in one hand.

And now? Well, the possibility of falling a little bit in love again with Andy was an attractive thought. I could feel my cheeks grow warm, and to cover my blush I pulled my hand away and dived deep, enjoying the pale green water as it slid around my body. A school of minnows silver-streaked across my path, leaving speckles of reflected light in their wake. I was alone in a beautiful, silent world that belonged only to me, until my lungs ached for air and I flip-flopped, shooting up toward the surface of the water.

I heard Kent yell, "Cannonball!" seconds before he slammed against me, driving me downward through the icy water of the lake into a tangle of vines that twisted around my ankles. My head was a fireball of pain, and my lungs burned with such agony, I thought they'd explode as I struggled desperately to get free.

Suddenly I became aware that the pain had gone,

3

and I was set apart—like a mildly curious bystander—watching the entire scene. Some of the kids dived from the float, managing together to tear through the vines and release my body. They laid it facedown on the float, and Andy—who had worked most summers as a lifeguard—grabbed my waist, hoisting me to let the water run from my open mouth. He quickly rolled me onto my back, placed his mouth over mine, and began to puff bursts of air into my lungs.

I moved closer, not wanting to look at this body I had left behind, yet at the same time not wanting to leave. I knew I had died, and it puzzled me that the others didn't know this too. I laid a hand on Andy's shoulder, even though I knew he couldn't feel it. "Poor Andy. Don't try. It's too late," I said, but of course he couldn't hear me.

Marcie wailed and struck at Kent with both fists. "You idiot! You stupid jerk!"

Kent kept sobbing. "I didn't know Sarah was under me when I jumped. Honest, I didn't know." I wanted to tell him that I didn't blame him, but I began to dream of lights and voices, and when my dream ended, I was in a hospital bed, amazed to see my mother and father bending over me.

"I'm still here," I whispered, bewildered by the direction my dream had taken. My parents hugged me and began to cry.

Later I held Andy tightly and said, "You saved my life," but I wasn't telling him the truth. Of course I was alive. I was here, with my family and my friends, as I'd always been; but at the same time I felt as though a part of me still inhabited another shadowy world.

4

I knew this because of the spirit.

I don't know exactly what to call it: a spirit, a presence, a wraith. It was invisible, it was soundless, yet I knew it was there, shadowing me in a quiet, almost gentle way.

At first I was frightened. Did you ever have the feeling that you were being watched and turn around quickly and find someone staring at you? Well, I'd turn, but no one would be there; yet I'd still have the creepy feeling that someone was present, someone whose eyes were still upon me.

I'd even reached out, trying to touch whatever might be there. "Who are you?" I'd whispered into the silence, but no one answered.

I didn't tell Mom or Dad about the presence. What could I say that wouldn't sound ridiculous and wouldn't cause Mom to worry about me? Besides, I began to get used to my invisible shadow. I don't remember exactly when or why I stopped being afraid, maybe when it occurred to me that this presence was like someone standing protectively by my side, someone who cared about me.

That's when I made a terrible mistake.

Marcie, Andy, Kent—all of us—were at Marcie's house one evening, and Kent began telling one of those weird murderer-with-an-iron-claw stories that's always supposed to have happened to a friend of a friend. Andy topped Kent's story with a gruesome ghost story, and we were laughing and acting so crazy that I suddenly said, "I'll tell you something that's really true! Listen to what's

5

been happening to me!" Like a fool, I blurted out the whole story about the spirit who shadowed me.

Nobody laughed. When I finished, their glances slid away. It was easy to see what they were thinking. Sarah's weird. She's strange. My face flushed hotly, and I wondered if it was possible to die from embarrassment. Why had I been so stupid as to tell them? To make everything even worse, I felt as though I'd somehow betrayed the invisible spirit.

Marcie finally broke the silence by saying, "Sarah, something's wrong. It's creepy. Have you told your parents what you told us?"

"No," I said. I tried a laugh but couldn't make it. "And I wish now I hadn't told you."

A little frown dipped between Marcie's eyebrows as she said, "I really think you should tell your parents."

I did, hoping, I guess, that I'd get reassurance from Mom; but it didn't happen that way. Mom immediately took me to Dr. Clark, our family doctor, and I had to repeat the story to him.

Dr. Clark was the first person who had listened to me calmly. "There've been some studies made about this—what you might call a haunted feeling," he told us.

"What do you mean?" Mom's voice was high-pitched, and she gripped the edge of her chair.

"A number of children who've been on the brink of death and recovered have claimed they were being followed by an invisible presence. One of them was the author, Edith Wharton."

I got hung up on the word *children* and complained. "I'm not a child."

6

"You're only sixteen, Sarah, so you're not an adult," Dr. Clark answered. "Now stop interrupting so I can tell you the rest. The author of one study believes that some children who have had a near-death experience made contact with another dimension and are reluctant to lose this contact, so they become more sensitive or intuitive to what you might call otherworldly beings."

Mom gasped. What he said scared me too. "Are you talking ghosts?" I asked him.

He shook his head. "I'm just trying to tell you that other people have experienced what you have, that you're not alone in having these unusual sensations. I thought it might help you to know that."

It didn't help. I wanted control over my own mind. I didn't want to be some kind of weird link between two worlds. *Weird Sarah. Haunted Sarah.* I shivered.

"What do we do about this?" Mom's voice hit another high note, and she gripped my hand.

Dr. Clark reached over and patted her shoulder. "For one thing, Dorothy, don't worry," he said. "These odd experiences that have been bothering Sarah will eventually fade out and disappear as the trauma recedes."

"As the trauma recedes?" I asked. "What does that mean?"

"In your case, probably when you stop reliving your fear of drowning," he told me.

"I almost drowned. How can I *not* remember that?"

"I didn't say 'remember.' I said, 'relive.' "

"Does Sarah need counseling? Some kind of therapy?" Mom asked.

"I don't think so," Dr. Clark said as he smiled at me. "I think she needs to stay busy with her friends. Have fun, go swimming again."

It was hard to hold back a shudder. Go swimming? Never!

During the weeks that followed, Mom and Dad were strong and steady, as they'd always been, but sometimes a little scared-rabbit look flickered in Mom's eyes, and I wondered what she thought—*really* thought—about what was going on in my mind.

I wished I knew myself.

Sometimes I'd groan, wondering, *Why did this happen to me? And why had I been dumb enough to talk about it?*

It was obvious that what I had told them made my friends uncomfortable. Marcie was the only one who stood by me; but sometimes, when we were alone together, watching TV or walking to the mall, even she'd get jumpy. "Is everything okay?" she'd ask, and I'd wonder if she was afraid of the spirit or of me.

The passage of time helped the memories to fade, and even though sometimes at night the water closed over my head and I awoke from my nightmare struggling for air, the dreams came less and less frequently.

I tried to convince myself that everything soon would be as it once was. I wouldn't let myself think beyond that point. And I was surprised when one day it dawned on me that my secret wraith had slipped away. I was even more surprised when I discovered that it was more like a loss than a victory. *I had to get rid of you,* I

8

thought. *I had to stay in control.* But it wasn't there to hear me.

"Everything will be back to normal now," I convinced myself, but I was wrong.

Dad got the promotion he'd been hoping for, which meant he'd make a couple of moves, the first one to his company's Houston office. He brought home a bottle of champagne, and his face shone as he told us his news.

I wanted to cry, to scream, "We can't leave Springdale! This is our home!" But everything had changed, and it wouldn't be our home any longer.

Dad said to Mom, "I'll have to report to the new office by next week. If you can take care of winding up the details here, I'll do the house-hunting for us in Houston."

For just an instant Mom had looked wistfully at her collection of potted plants in the sunny bay window. "Make it a beautiful house," she said.

"I promise," he answered.

It wasn't until later, after I'd rushed to Marcie's house to tell her we'd be leaving, that I gave in to my tears. Marcie cried, too, but at the same time her eyes held a look of almost giddy relief—the same kind of look someone gets when she's called on to solve a tough problem in geometry and makes it.

"Maybe I can come back next summer for a visit," I told her, "and in the meantime we can write lots of letters."

"Sure," Marcie agreed, "but you know me. I'm not much of a letter writer."

My silent shadow had vanished, but so had my

friends. I wanted to blame the shadow, but I couldn't. I knew that the pain from the loneliness that smothered me was my own fault for telling. Was I totally free of any link to another world? I couldn't be sure. But no matter what happened to me in the future, I'd keep it to myself, even keep it from Mom and Dad. I'd never be humiliated like that again.

Chapter One

As we stood outside the empty, contemporary-style house that was to be our Houston home, Mom said, "Frank, I can't believe it. This neighborhood, this house —how can we afford it?"

Dad grinned. "Trust me," he said. He pulled the house key from his pocket and told us, "The electricity's on, so the air-conditioning should have cooled the house. Just give me a few minutes to open drapes and let in the sunlight before you come inside. I want you to see the house at its best." He sprinted off, disappearing through the large front door.

Mom glanced to each side at the large houses on the street, then back to our house. "I really didn't expect anything like this," she said. She clasped my hand, the way she would when I was very young and we'd cross the street, but I could tell that this time she was the one needing help. "It's not much like our house in Springdale," she added.

"It's a lot bigger," I said, not knowing how to reassure her.

"Sarah," Mom said, "I know it's hard to move away from friends, from the home you're used to. It's—"

I interrupted brusquely. "It's okay, Mom. We don't have to talk about it."

But she finished the sentence she'd begun. "It's hard for me too," she murmured. Mom gave my hand a little squeeze and raised her voice as though determined to be cheerful. "Your father's had enough time to get things ready. Let's see what our house looks like on the inside."

She threw open the door and stepped into the entry hall, and I followed. "Oh!" Mom said, staring up at the high ceiling. "This is beautiful!" But I couldn't move. I felt as though I'd been sucked into a cold, smothering mist that surged forward, its thudding heartbeat racing, pounding against my forehead like hammer blows. The echo of a scream beat against my mind, and I gasped in panic.

The front door slammed shut behind me. "Sarah," Mom said, "what is it? You're trembling."

Mom's words echoed loudly in the empty hallway, shattering the mist, and it retreated. Hovering, waiting, its dark shreds silently clung to the walls.

I didn't stop to think. "It's this house," I whispered. "Can't you feel it?"

Mom's eyes widened in fear, and she struggled to keep her voice steady. "There's nothing wrong with this

12

house," she said. "Whatever you think you may feel, well . . . it's—"

With a shudder I finished her sentence. "I know, Mom. You're trying to figure out the tactful way to say that you think the problem is me. I'm sorry I said anything. I shouldn't have."

She put an arm around me and gave me a comforting, strengthening hug; but I heard tension bite through her words. "Sweetheart, if you felt something frightening . . . well, couldn't it be just a trick of your imagination?"

This was not like the other time. There was something horrible here in this house, and it had reached out and touched me. I wanted to scream, "Don't do this to me! I don't want to be a link to some other world! Leave me alone!"

But I tried to stay calm, nodded agreement, and said, "You're right. It was just my imagination."

Mom stroked my hair back from my face with her free hand. "Oh, Sarah, I thought those feelings you had were over."

"They are," I insisted, hating myself for being different, for being strange.

I heard Dad enter the house through the back door and cross the kitchen. "Dorothy!" he called.

"Don't tell Dad what I said, please," I whispered to Mom. "I'd rather just forget what happened."

"If you're sure," she said, and I could tell that she'd like to forget it too.

"I'm sure."

Dad strode through the dining room to join us in the

front entry hall. He wasn't a handsome man, but he was tall and broad-shouldered, and at that moment he looked so pleased with himself, he couldn't keep from grinning. His attention was focused completely upon the house, and he gently ran a finger up the smooth wood molding around the tall window at the left side of the front door, examining it carefully.

"How do you like the place?" he asked, and without waiting for an answer, he added proudly, "I did all right with my house-hunting. You'll have to admit it."

"It's a beautiful house, Ron," Mom answered. "I can't believe you picked it up for such a low price." She smiled up at him with such admiration that his grin grew wider.

Mom—with her shaggy salt-and-pepper hair and her figure, which was too flat on top and a little too wide at the bottom—never would have won a beauty contest, but Dad often looked at her as though he knew she was the most marvelous person who'd ever entered his life.

He pretended to preen a bit. "That's one more point to my credit. Evelyn Pritchard, the real-estate agent I told you about, the one who helped me house-hunt, lives right next door. She said that it was very important to her to have good neighbors, so she was tickled pink when I made an offer on the house."

Mom giggled. "Your agent took a lot on trust," she said. "What if you'd had a mean wife and horrible children who zoomed around the neighborhood at midnight on dirt bikes and threw rocks at cats?"

Dad laughed. "I told Evelyn all about you and Sarah, and she's eager to meet you." Impatiently he added,

14

"You haven't set foot out of the entry hall. Wait until you see the rest of the house."

Mom took my hand and we followed Dad. As we walked through the rooms our voices echoed, bouncing off the high ceilings and the bare walls. But there were other voices. The house seemed filled with whispers, and twice I turned, almost expecting to see someone behind me.

Mom and Dad didn't seem to hear them. They chattered on about where to put the freezer and if the microwave should go here or there as though there were just the three of us present.

Get out of here! In my mind I shouted at the whisperer, *This is our house now, and you don't belong here! Go away! Leave me alone!*

The sudden silence startled me. The spirits had listened to me. I'd won. I gave a long, grateful sigh of relief.

I caught up to Mom and Dad, trying hard to concentrate on what Dad was showing us. He had kept his promise to Mom to find her a beautiful house. The front and backyards of this house were shaded with pines and dotted with late summer flowers. The ceilings were high, and there was lots of glass, so that the rooms were bright with dappled sunlight.

"They've left the draperies," Mom said. She fingered them and smiled. "Look at that. They're thermal-lined. That's going to help keep the air-conditioning bills down during this August heat."

Dad opened a door at the far end of the kitchen. "The agent called this the maid's room and bath. We could use it for storage, or you might think of something else." Mom peeked inside, and I had barely enough time for a glance before Dad said, "Come on. You haven't seen the master bedroom. It's downstairs, too, and it even has a whirlpool in the bathtub."

"I still can't believe what I'm seeing," Mom said. "How did you manage this?"

"It was way under market price," Dad told her.

"Why?" I asked.

He shrugged. "It could be any one of a number of reasons. Houston's economy has been down for a few years. That could do it. Also, I was told that the people who owned the house got a divorce. I hired an inspector, and he reported that the structure was fine, the foundation wasn't cracked, and everything checked out nicely. The previous owners had even installed a new roof and air conditioner when the house went on the market." He chuckled. "I made an offer even a little lower than the asking price, and the owners actually accepted it."

"You're wonderful," Mom said.

Divorce? Unhappiness? Maybe this was what I was picking up. Nothing otherworldly about that. I felt a little better. "Were either of the owners living in the house at the time you looked at it?" I asked.

"No," Dad said. "According to Evelyn, about a year and a half ago they moved out."

"Why did they both move?"

"Don't ask me," Dad said. "Maybe the house held too many unhappy memories and neither one wanted to live in it. Whatever the reason, it worked out to our advantage. The house was standing empty, and the owners

16

were eager to unload it and get out of making double house payments."

"Why all the questions?" Mom asked me.

I shrugged. "Just nosy," I answered.

"Wait until you see your room upstairs," Dad told me. "There are two big, attractive bedrooms and a bath. You'll have the entire floor to yourself. The back bedroom even has a balcony that overlooks a small courtyard."

He led the way to the entry hall and the stairs. I steeled myself, but the horrifying presence didn't return.

"The hall tile and the carpet on the stairs all look new," Mom said.

"It is," Dad answered. "Evelyn said so."

I touched my fingertips to the gleaming white surface of the walls. "I wonder why they painted here but not in the other rooms we looked at."

"As far as I've seen, the other rooms probably didn't need it," Mom said, "and of course there's wallpaper in the kitchen and on the long wall in the master bedroom and—"

"Come on!" Dad said, interrupting. He was already halfway up the stairs, eager to continue the tour, so we followed him to an upper hallway, which led to two large bedrooms connected by a bath. He was right. They were big, beautiful rooms, but I paused at the doorway to the bedroom, which faced the front of the house, driven back by the cold that permeated this room. "Too much air-conditioning in here," I said, and chose the back bedroom with its balcony and view.

"There you have it," he said. His eyes twinkled as he waited for further praise.

Mom was right there on cue, and I followed with, "It's the prettiest room I've ever had." That part was true, but I was still uncomfortable with this house. I still didn't understand what I'd felt and heard. I took a long breath, determined never to think of it again. Whatever it was had gone, hadn't it? Of course it had. I'd ordered it to leave, and it had obeyed. The sudden silence had been my answer. Hadn't it?

My eyes were drawn toward the doorway to the other upstairs bedroom, and I shivered, wrapping my arms across my chest as I remembered the cold.

The doorbell rang, and I jumped; but Mom said, "It must be the movers," and we rushed downstairs to let them in.

The rest of the day I avoided bumping into furniture and packing boxes, helped check out of the hotel where we had spent the night, went driving in search of hamburgers, and tried to wash dishes and put them away as quickly as they were being unpacked.

Finally, long after the movers had left, Mom flopped into a chair and said, "That's enough. I'm exhausted. We'll finish tomorrow. Let's shower and get into clean clothes and go looking for a restaurant."

Dad looked at his watch. "Evelyn seemed so glad to have us as neighbors, I had sort of thought she'd come by." He shrugged and added, "Remember when we moved into our house in Springdale? Claire came from next door with a casserole."

18

"Claire was special," Mom said. "I miss her. It's hard to leave friends."

For a moment her eyes blurred with tears. I don't know why it surprised me. I should have realized that Mom would miss her friends just as much as I would miss mine. My throat ached, and I tried to keep from thinking about Marcie and Andy and all the others.

Dad turned to me. "I haven't met any of the neighbors, except for Evelyn Pritchard, but I saw a couple of teenagers on the street the first time I came here. They looked to be about your age, Sarah. I think one of them is Evelyn's daughter."

I just shrugged, too tired to care.

Dad looked from me to Mom and said, "Is anyone here as hungry as I am? What'll it be? Chinese? Mexican? Barbecue?"

Mom perked up and struggled out of the chair. "Do you suppose we can find a good Hunan restaurant nearby?"

"Count me out," I told them. "I'm too tired to be hungry."

"You've got to eat," Mom said.

"Then could you bring back something? Shrimp lo mein? I'd really like to finish unpacking my clothes and putting my bedroom together. Point out the box of sheets and I'll make your bed for you too."

"But, Sarah—" Mom began.

Dad silenced her with a look and said, "Sounds like a good trade. Come on, Dorothy. Let's get ready."

Making the beds was no problem. Mom was a stickler for marking boxes and making sure they were carried to the right rooms, so I finished that task soon after they left. I began work on my room, and it didn't take long before my clothes were hanging in the closet, my suitcase was on the shelf, and even my special mementos were in place on top of the chest of drawers.

I picked up the photos I'd framed—Marcie and me on the school steps, Kent making faces over Barbie's shoulder, Andy frowning sternly down from his lifeguard tower at the pool. My chest began to hurt, and the tears I'd held back exploded. I flung myself on the bed and cried until there were no more tears and my body shuddered with dry sobs.

I was exhausted, numb, half awake, half asleep. I began to pull the silence around me, as though it were a comfortable, old down quilt. But the house was *not* silent. Softly, from the other room, I heard an echo of my tears.

I raised my head. I could hear the sound more clearly now. "Mom?" I called out. It had to be Mom.

Mom didn't answer, but the pitiful sobbing continued. It was a woman who was crying, and her tears weren't a noisy storm, as mine were, but those of someone who had given in to despair.

I scrambled from the bed, following the sound, until I was standing at the head of the stairs, looking down past the railing into the entry hall.

Enough early-evening light streamed through the window next to the front door to yellow the walls, spreading its glow across a spindly, antique table I'd never seen before. On it, lying on its side, was an unfamiliar crystal vase of early spring sweet peas, spilled and dripping onto white marblelike tiles.

The sound of crying stopped. Then, out of the silence came a whisper so heartbreaking, so desperate, that it tugged me forward: "*¡Ayúdame! ¡Ayúdame!*"

My heart was pounding so loudly that I could hear it in my ears as I moved closer to the railing, bent over, and looked straight down.

Directly below me, under the brown-red splattered walls, lay a pool of blood.

Chapter Two

I closed my eyes, wondering if I was going to faint. It was hard to breathe, and my legs couldn't hold me up. I dropped down so hard on the top step that my eyes flew open, and I knew immediately that whatever vision I'd glimpsed had gone. The freshly painted walls were stark and clean, gleaming under their wash of mellow sunlight. The stair wall under the banister was solid, no railings to peer through, so I leaned my head against it and took a couple of long, steadying breaths.

It was clear to me now that for some reason I was still linked to another world. Why me? I groaned, mumbling under my breath that it wasn't fair. My other experience had been peaceful, at least, but this one was terrifying. Should I tell Mom and Dad about it?

No! The answer was so urgent and so positive, for an instant I wondered if it came from my own mind or someone else's. I squeezed my eyes shut tightly. What was happening to me? Had I become Strange Sarah, the weirdo who deals with ghosts? Mom had been scared to death by what had happened to me before. How would she react to this? I shuddered. I couldn't tell my parents, not until I understood what was going on. The word I had heard still echoed in my mind: *Ayúdame.* I knew enough Spanish to be familiar with that call for help. I ached for the woman who had cried out with such desperation. Had she once called, and no one heard?

A thought hit me with such impact that I shuddered. Maybe I hadn't picked up her cry to someone else. Maybe she had been calling to me!

At the foot of the stairs, next to the front door, was a two-foot-wide floor-to-ceiling window. I could see my parents' car come up the driveway and make a sharp right-angle turn into the garage, which was at the front of the house. I managed to struggle to my feet and stumbled down the stairs to open the door for them, shivering against the unnatural chill in the entry hall. A house so open to the sun and heat, and yet so cold.

"The restaurant we found is really good," Mom said as she thrust a white paper bag into my hands and began to herd me toward the kitchen. I wondered if my eyes showed what I'd been through. Fortunately Mom didn't look at me closely enough to notice. "I had some of the shrimp lo mein, too, and you'll love it," she said. "Hurry up. Eat it while it's still hot."

While I cleared off a spot at one end of the table, Mom chattered on. "I love this neighborhood. Everything's so handy, and there's a swimming pool and tennis courts and—"

I tuned her out, still trembling inside from the vision I'd seen and the voice I'd heard. Dr. Clark had said some people who'd had near-death experiences had found themselves more sensitive and intuitive to otherworldly beings. Was this why I'd heard the cry for help? But why had the woman chosen to contact me? There must be a reason.

In our still messy, warm, and cozy kitchen, the scene I'd heard and seen a short time ago seemed no more than a dream. I couldn't understand it or what it had to do with me, and I hoped with all my heart it would never return.

■

I was exhausted, so in spite of what had happened, I slept well all through the night.

The next morning I pulled my bicycle out from the boxes and crates piled along one side of the garage and set out to take a close look at this part of Houston. Even with its huge shade trees and thick green lawns, the city was so different from Springdale. For one thing, there were no hills to coast down. I suddenly wondered if I were to look from a window at the top of one of downtown Houston's highest buildings, could I see all the way home? I stopped to wipe the blur of tears from my eyes. Springdale, Missouri, was no longer home. This was. Slowly I retraced my route and turned into our cul-de-sac street.

A plump girl, with hair the color of pale lemonade, got up from the shaded porch step of the Colonial-style house next to ours. She waved with one hand as she

24

tugged down her shorts with the other. Her T-shirt was purple, her shorts were red, and her hair was tied back by a faded green scarf. As I pulled my bike to a stop she came to meet me. "Hi!" she called. "I'm Dee Dee Pritchard. We're next-door neighbors. I saw you leave on your bike, so I waited for you."

"I'm Sarah Darnell," I answered.

She giggled. "I know that, and I know we're the same age. Believe me, Mom finds out *everything.* If you've got some time, come on in. We can get a Coke or something. I can fill you in on stuff, like the high school and . . . You *are* going to Memorial High, aren't you?"

"I don't know." Before Dee Dee began again, I said, "I've got to put my bike away and tell Mom where I am. Why don't you come with me? By this time there'll be ice in the refrigerator, and I know we've got some soft drinks in one of the packing boxes."

A peculiar look flickered in Dee Dee's eyes. Curiosity? Fear? While I was trying to figure it out, she said slowly, "Okay. Sure. I'd like to see what the inside of your house looks like. It's real modern, isn't it? I mean, sort of like those pictures of rooms with wide, plain walls in *Architectural Digest.*"

"I guess so," I answered, but I was puzzled. "You live right next door. Haven't you been inside the house?"

"No," she answered. "Oh, I sneaked over and looked in the window by the front door when—" She caught herself and quickly shifted the subject. "Have you got a cat or a dog?" she asked. "We've got a dog. We named him after my Uncle Billy. He's really stupid—the dog not Uncle Billy—and a big pain when he's tearing up a

25

flower bed or some dumb thing like that, but we're all crazy about him, and . . ."

By the time Dee Dee wound down, we had reached the front door. She stopped talking and just stared as I opened it.

"We've got a calico cat named Dinky," I told Dee Dee. "She's boarding at the vet's. Mom thought it would be easier for her while we were moving in." I could see that Dee Dee wasn't paying attention to anything I was saying.

I led the way into the house, and Dee Dee followed slowly. She stood very still just inside the entry hall as I closed the front door behind us, and I could swear that for a moment she stopped breathing. The pale blue pupils of her eyes darted back and forth as she tried to scan every inch of the entry hall.

"The hall's kind of plain right now," I told her, "but Mom has a big potted plant and a large picture that should look good right over there."

With an effort Dee Dee looked directly into my eyes. "I'm ready for that Coke," she said. "Which way is the kitchen?"

Dad had left for his office already, but Mom was still at home. Mom had worked for years as a legal secretary, but she planned to give herself a month's vacation before she started job-hunting. I introduced Dee Dee, and while we were finding the Cokes, Mom asked her about the people who had lived here before we bought the house.

"Holt. That was their name, wasn't it? Mr. and Mrs. Martin Holt," Mom said.

26

"They weren't very neighborly," Dee Dee added quickly. "None of the neighbors knew them very well."

"Oh," Mom said. "I guess I just wondered a little about them—if they had children, things like that."

"They had one boy." Dee Dee's voice dropped almost to a whisper. "He wasn't very friendly to most of us. Except he was to a guy down the block—Eric Hendrickson. They were friends."

I handed Dee Dee a Coke and a glass filled with ice cubes and motioned toward a chair. She sat on the edge and shifted and squirmed. I was pretty sure it wasn't the chair that was making her uncomfortable.

"You're bound to meet Eric soon," Dee Dee said to me. "He likes pretty girls."

"Will I like him?"

She shrugged. "He's okay, I guess, but he did stand up Cyndi Baker once, and she hates him. They were going to a dance at the country club her father belongs to, and she'd bought a new dress and—" I heard Dee Dee shift gears. She was back in safe territory again.

"If you girls will excuse me, I'm going to run to the grocery store for a few minutes," Mom said.

"You're leaving?" Dee Dee was half out of her chair.

Mom threw Dee Dee a puzzled look, rummaged under a pile of rumpled packing paper for her keys and purse, waved good-bye, and left.

Dee Dee turned to me and asked, "Why don't we go to my house?" That strange expression was on her face again.

I sat down beside her and poured a little more Coke

27

into my glass. "We just started these. We can stay here until we finish, can't we?"

"Uh, yes. I guess so," she answered.

As I looked over at Dee Dee she deliberately brightened. She took a big slurp of Coke, fought back a burp, blinked, and said, "Tell me, do you have any pets? A dog or a cat?"

For an instant her question took me by surprise, but I remembered Dee Dee's wary look as we entered the house. I knew at the time she wasn't paying attention to what I'd been saying. "We have a cat. She's still boarding at the vet's," I answered, and patiently repeated everything I'd told her about Dinky.

"I'll tell you about Memorial High," Dee Dee said. "There's this 'in' group, of course, but forget them. Who needs them, huh? I like people who are interesting because they're different, don't you?" She began to relate a funny story about some guy she knew at school, but I tuned *her* out. That horrible experience I'd had the day before wasn't a hallucination, and it wasn't something growing from my imagination. There *was* something strange about this house, and Dee Dee knew what it was.

How was I going to get her to tell me?

"—so that's what he said, and he never knew why he got in trouble!" Dee Dee laughed, and I laughed with her. I wondered what the joke was.

"You said you hadn't been in this house before. Would you like to see the rest of it?" I asked.

She stiffened but finally answered, "Sure. Why not?"

Dee Dee tagged closely after me. She didn't give a second thought to the whirlpool in the master bathroom.

28

The Pritchards had one too. "Same builder. He did everything on this block," Dee Dee said. "Our Colonial's probably the largest. Mom went nuts over those pillars across the front of the house. Frankly I think it's too *Gone with the Wind* inside and out. It should have come with Rhett Butler."

She continued to babble until we crossed the entry hall and headed up the stairs. She not only fell silent but also seemed to be holding her breath. The guest bedroom was cluttered with boxes we hadn't sorted through yet, but my room was fairly well put together.

"Good." Dee Dee gave a relieved sigh. "You've got the back bedroom. Adam had the front."

I whirled and faced her. "What are you talking about?"

She looked as though she'd been caught cheating on an exam. "N-nothing," she said, stammering. "I was just rattling on. Everybody says I talk too much. You've learned that about me by this time."

"Who's Adam?"

She shrugged. "Adam Holt."

"I thought you hadn't been in this house."

"I haven't. Mom described the house to us when she listed it for sale."

I leaned against the chest of drawers and said, "Okay. Now tell me about Adam Holt."

"Adam ignored me," Dee Dee said, "which was just as well." I must have looked puzzled because she quickly added, "He was very charming when he felt like it. He was . . ." She hesitated, searching for the right word. "Seductive."

29

"Seductive?" I echoed. "That's a strange way to describe him."

"Adam was strange, period," she insisted. "He wouldn't even bother to speak to most of the people on the block." She sneaked a quick, defensive glance at herself in the mirror over the chest of drawers and added, "It wasn't just me."

"But 'seductive'? What did you mean by that?"

"Adam could make girls fall all over him." She leaned closer to me, although there was no one around to hear, and murmured, "There was a story about a girl he raped. At least she said he did, but Adam insisted she was lying."

"Was he arrested?"

"No. She had a reputation, so it all kind of died down." She stopped and looked at me helplessly. "That's all I can tell you about Adam."

"Then tell me why you're afraid of this house."

She gasped, and her eyes widened. "I'm not," she insisted, but it was easy to see that she was lying.

Bluntly I said, "There's something frightening about this house, isn't there, Dee Dee? I don't know what it is, but you do, don't you?"

Dee Dee laughed nervously. "I don't know why you think that," she said, but her eyes didn't meet mine. As she spoke, she moved toward the door. "Come on over and meet my mom. She said she had an appointment at eleven, so she'll still be home."

Silently I followed Dee Dee, making sure I locked the front door as we left the house. By the time we crossed our double lawns and reached her home, she was once again her outgoing, talkative self.

30

Whispers from the Dead

I quickly discovered what she meant by *Gone with the Wind* decor. There was an artfully arranged clutter of tiny, enameled boxes, porcelain birds, family photographs, and all sorts of small odds and ends on every table of every size throughout what I could see of the Pritchards' home. The deep blue brocade draperies in the large living room were shirred, ruffled, and sashed; and a gigantic portrait of a couple from Civil War days hung over the fireplace.

"Your relatives?" I asked.

Dee Dee shook her head. "Mom picked up the painting in some antique shop in New Orleans. She bought it because the woman's gown matched our drapes."

"You didn't meet Billy," she said, and pointed to an old, nondescript dog who was snoozing at one end of the sofa. Billy flicked an ear but didn't bother to open his eyes.

I heard footsteps behind me and turned, prepared to greet Dee Dee's mother, but a small woman in a white uniform nodded and smiled at us as she removed two used coffee cups from the arrangement on the ornate mahogany coffee table. With all the clutter, I wondered how she'd found them.

"Lupita," Dee Dee said, "this is one of our new neighbors, Sarah Darnell. She and her parents just moved into the Holt house."

Lupita's eyes opened wide and her lips parted. Her words came out in a bare whisper. *"Buenos días."*

"I'm not going to keep teaching you English if you won't use it," Dee Dee told her. "Now . . . how do you say it in English?"

31

"G-glad to meet you," Lupita said, stammering. She seemed awfully nervous.

"I'm glad to meet you too," I answered.

As Lupita scurried out of the room Dee Dee sighed. "She's in this country illegally, of course. Mom hires illegals so she won't have to pay as much. Maybe if Immigration offers amnesty again, Lupita will make it, but until then she either works here for someone like Mom or goes back to Mexico."

"Is that why she seems frightened of me?"

Dee Dee glanced at me sharply for an instant, then shrugged. "I don't think you frightened her. Lupita's been scared of being caught and sent back ever since she arrived in Houston five years ago, but she's used to Mom entertaining people here. She knows that some of Mom's friends hire illegals, too, so she's in no danger from them."

"You're teaching her English?"

Dee Dee grinned. "Yes. Just between you and me and Lupita, if she learns to speak and read and write English, she can get a better job than this one."

I grinned back. I was beginning to like Dee Dee.

"Come on," she said. "Let's go and find my mom."

Just then Mrs. Pritchard strode into the room, briefcase in hand, and beamed at me. Her handshake was firm and quick, but she clung to my hand for just an instant, as though she were reluctant to let go. "You must be Sarah," she said. "Your father was right to brag about you. You're a lovely girl. All that dark curly hair and those gorgeous green eyes!" She leaned closer. "My goodness, there's a ring of gold around the green. Very dramatic! Isn't that supposed to mean something special? That you're fey? Attuned to things the rest of us aren't?"

I gasped as a shiver wiggled down my spine, but she didn't seem to notice.

"I would have come over to pay a call, but I had some clients who had to be taken care of. You know how it is," she said. "But I'll be over as soon as I can possibly make it. I can't wait to meet your mother. She's going to love the neighborhood. Everyone is so friendly. We're all so happy that you and your family live here now."

She kissed Dee Dee's forehead and smiled at me again. She had a radiant smile. She was a taller, trimmer, much more polished version of Dee Dee.

As she left, her high heels clicking on the marble tiles in the Pritchard entry hall, I said to Dee Dee, "I like your mother."

"Everybody does," she answered. She looked at her watch. "I'm working the noon-to-two shift as lifeguard down at the pool. Why don't you put on a bathing suit and come with me?"

I couldn't help shuddering.

"What's the matter?" Dee Dee asked. "Don't you know how to swim?"

"I'm a good swimmer," I managed to say.

"You looked at me the same way you would if I asked if you'd like to catch rattlesnakes."

I decided to be open with Dee Dee—about why I wouldn't swim, that is. "In May I got caught in some vines at the bottom of a lake. I nearly drowned. I've been afraid to go into the water ever since."

Even though her eyes widened in surprise, she didn't miss a beat. "You're missing a lot of fun," she said. "You're supposed to go right back into the water, to face up to your fears. Didn't anybody tell you that?"

"My doctor did."

"Well?"

"I had to—well, work out other problems first."

The wary look in her eyes was so much like Marcie's had been that it scared me. I didn't want Dee Dee to think I was strange, too, so I blurted out, "Your face shows everything you're thinking, Dee Dee. You don't have to worry about me. The problems had to do with the near drowning. I almost died, and— Oh, it's a long story."

Dee Dee smiled. "My father told me never to play poker. Everybody in the game would be able to tell if I had a good hand or was bluffing." Her glance flicked in the direction of our house. "I tell you what. When you want to go swimming again, I'll go with you. I'll be right at your side, so you won't need to be afraid. I'm a good swimmer, and I'm a good lifeguard too. A lot better than that snooty Richard Ailey, who's head lifeguard." She launched into another story, and by the time she reached the end we were both at ease with each other again.

We sauntered toward the front door with the usual "I'll call you later."

"Come over whenever you want."

A shadow moved behind Dee Dee, catching my eye. Lupita was peering at me, her eyes dark with a desperate concern. As my glance met hers she quickly turned away, but I saw her surreptitiously cross herself.

"What's wrong? What do you know that I don't know?" I wanted to shout at Dee Dee and Lupita.

But Dee Dee was saying, "I'm going to be late, and Richard is going to kill me!"

The door shut, and I reluctantly trudged toward my own house with the fear that something evil was there waiting for the right moment, waiting for me.

I hoped with all my heart that Mom was home.

Chapter Three

As I closed the front door the house settled uncomfortably around me. I hurried nervously toward the kitchen, toward the sound of Mom opening and shutting cabinet doors, and burst into the warmth and sunlight that streamed through the wide window over the sink.

Mom straightened and looked surprised. "Where's Dee Dee?"

"She works each afternoon for two hours as lifeguard at the neighborhood pool." I began to poke through the cabinet. "What did you get for us to eat? I'm starving."

"How about a make-your-own sandwich? There's some Colby cheese and sliced ham."

"Want me to make one for you?"

Mom sighed. "Thanks. I'd love it. No ham in mine. Just cheese and lettuce."

She plopped into a chair and rested her chin on her hands. "I met one of our neighbors in the grocery store.

36

Her name's Margaret Taylor, and she lives in the corner house. I'd seen her taking her newspaper in yesterday, so when I recognized her in the grocery store, I went over to say hello and introduce myself."

There was an oddly strained tone in Mom's voice, so I stopped slapping mayonnaise on the bread and looked at her. "Wasn't she friendly?"

"I suppose she was friendly enough," Mom answered. "I'm just a little puzzled by the way she acted. She seemed somewhat embarrassed."

"Why would she be embarrassed?"

"I can't imagine. Our conversation was short. She told me what a wonderful friend and neighbor Evelyn Pritchard is, and how everyone on the block would do anything for her, and how she hoped we'd soon feel the same way about her.

"I didn't know quite how to answer that, so I said I was looking forward to meeting Evelyn and invited Margaret to come by for a cup of coffee. She got so flustered, she dropped the box of cereal she was holding and insisted that I visit *her* instead. She said something about telephoning me soon, and that was that."

I stumbled across the kitchen, slid into the chair opposite Mom, and reached across the table to grasp her hands. "Mom," I said, "there's nothing wrong with Mrs. Whoever-she-is. There's something wrong with this house."

Mom gave a little gasp of surprise and asked, "Sarah, what are you talking about?"

"I wish I knew. That neighbor you met isn't the only one who acts strange. Dee Dee does too. I could tell that

37

she was curious about what the house looked like inside, but even though she came in with me, she couldn't wait to get out of here and back to her own house."

"It doesn't make any sense," Mom said.

"Not to us, it doesn't, but it does to that neighbor, and it does to Dee Dee." I leaned back in my chair and sighed. I wished I could tell Mom what I'd felt in this house. Tentatively I tried a test. I wanted to see how Mom would react. "If there's something wrong with this house, how will we find out?"

Mom pushed back her chair and stood, appraising me. "There's nothing wrong with this house, Sarah," she said firmly. "It's a beautiful house. It's the most beautiful house we've ever lived in. Please, sweetheart, don't let your imagination—"

She stopped, and I hurried to say, "Mom, I'm okay. All right? You're the one who brought up the crazy way our neighbor was acting."

Mom's cheeks grew pink. "I'm sorry. I shouldn't have been thinking out loud." She smiled. "If you're not going to finish making those sandwiches, then I will."

"I'll do it." I jumped up and began washing the lettuce. It was obvious to me that there was some unhappy story connected with this house, and people who knew it were trying to keep it from us. Mom may have wanted to avoid finding out, but I had to know. *¡Ayúdame!* That desperate, pitiful call for help rushed back into my mind. Something in this house wanted me to know.

As soon as we finished our sandwiches I asked, "What would you like me to do next?"

Mom looked at me gratefully. "How about tackling

the little room and bath next to the kitchen? We put some of the empty moving boxes in there to get them out of the way. You could take them out to the garage and dust and sweep the room. We ought to be able to make good use of it. It might be a good place to put the desk and computer."

"Dad said it was a maid's room."

Mom laughed. "A live-in maid doesn't fit our budget."

She went back to her work with the cabinets, and I dragged the big packing boxes out of the maid's room and into the garage. When the room was empty of clutter, I stopped to examine it. "If we put bookshelves along the walls and a window seat under that one window, this would make a terrific library," I told Mom. "Wouldn't it be fun to have our own library? It could be sort of like the ones in British movies."

"It's a possibility," Mom said. She picked up a rag and a can of cleanser and added, "I'm going to give the bathrooms a thorough going-over. If you want me, I'll be upstairs."

I leaned against the wall of the small room, just inside the door that leads to the kitchen. I tried to visualize the bookcase-lined walls with a comfortable chair over there, maybe a lamp table. We could use the one with the nick in it that Mom almost gave to a garage sale. But the imaginary layout suddenly disappeared, and a film shimmered across my mind.

Shadows of objects, so softly blurred that I couldn't make them out, glowed and faded, pulsing like a heartbeat. The air in the room ruffled softly against my face, and I could smell warm skin and hair. Someone was close by.

¡Ayúdame! The word, vibrating with terror, blew like a cold breath against my cheek.

Trembling, gasping with fear, I reached out to steady myself against the wall. It was firm and solid. The mist vanished, and once again the room was still and bright, with dust motes lazily drifting inside the band of sunlight that streamed through the uncovered window.

"Who are you?" I managed to whisper to this invisible woman. "What do you want?"

The room was blank, as though the vision and the voice had never taken place. My fear slowly turned to anger. "I don't want to be involved in this. It's not fair. Why are you doing this to me?" I demanded.

No answer came, but I didn't need one. I'd just had more proof that the thread which tied me to an existence beyond this world had not yet been broken. I was still vulnerable, as though I were a link from one world to the next. Did I have to accept this? What were my choices? What was I going to do?

My knees wobbled, so I slid down the wall and sat cross-legged on the bare wooden floor. Was that voice a hallucination? No. It was too real. Those terrified, pitiful cries for help were directed at *me*.

I groaned and pressed my palms against my forehead. I wanted to be freed from all this, to be in control of my own mind. Okay, there was a way to handle it. I could tell Mom and Dad everything and ask for help. Maybe a psychiatrist could help me get rid of this spirit.

But how could I turn my back on those heartbreaking pleas? If I ignored them, what would that poor desperate woman do? Who would help her? I realized I could no more walk away from this unseen spirit than I could if she were flesh and blood standing before me, begging for my help.

But our contact would have to be kept secret. I couldn't risk people knowing. Remembering the look in Marcie's eyes, I knew what they'd think. I shivered, realizing what the consequences might be. Did I have enough courage to carry this through?

Deliberately I made the choice.

I put my hands into my lap, straightened my shoulders, and stared into the room, wanting the woman to make contact again. "Listen to me, whoever you are," I said. "I promise to try to help you, but I can't help you this way. I need to know what happened to you. I need to know who you are. If you want me to help you, then *you've* got to help *me*. Do you understand?"

I waited tensely, almost afraid to breathe, but there was only silence.

I heard the doorbell and Mom's footsteps as she answered it. "Sarah!" she called. "Dee Dee's here."

Staggering to my feet, I dusted off my shorts, tugged my T-shirt into place, and gave one last look around the empty, quiet room. Nothing. "Coming!" I yelled.

It wasn't just Dee Dee who had come to visit. I followed the sound of voices into the den and saw a guy who was a couple of inches shorter than me standing next to Dee Dee. She'd tied her damp hair back from her face, and her skin still glowed from the sun at the pool.

"Hi, Sarah," Dee Dee said. "This is Eric Hendrickson."

Eric studied me so intently, I stared back, hoping he'd get the message to cut it out. He wasn't bad-looking, but not great-looking, either. His tan was blotchy, red-streaked across the bridge of his nose and cheeks, and his short-cropped hair was sun-bleached. He was dressed in white shorts and shirt and carried a tennis racket. I wondered what kind of nut would play tennis during the hottest part of an August day.

"Before I get back to work, would any of you like something cold to drink?" Mom asked.

"Thanks. I could use a beer," Eric said.

"No," Mom answered. "No beer."

"I'm eighteen," Eric said.

"No beer," Mom repeated with a smile. "There are soft drinks in the refrigerator. If you'd like, Sarah can get them for you." She left.

"That was real smart, Eric," Dee Dee said sarcastically.

"Hey, what's the matter with you, Chubby?" Eric complained. "She asked, didn't she?"

"You're a clod," Dee Dee muttered.

This was awful. I tried to distract them from their argument by asking, "Why are we just standing here? Why don't we sit down?"

Dee Dee curled on one end of the sofa, as far away from Eric as she could get. He flopped and slumped, his muscular legs stretched out into the room. "I saw you yesterday when your family was moving in," Eric said to me. "You gonna go to Memorial?"

"I guess," I answered, "if that's where everybody around here goes to high school."

"Some of the kids go to private schools—St. Agnes, St. John's, Kinkaid," Dee Dee said.

"What do you think of the house?" Eric asked me. His expression was so wide-eyed with innocence, it looked fake. I got the feeling he knew it. What was with him?

Dee Dee glared at Eric. "That's a stupid question. Why don't we talk about movies? Has anybody seen that new horror one? The one that takes place in a cemetery?"

"It's not a stupid question. I really want to know what Sarah thinks of the house." A trace of a smile flickered around his mouth. "Why don't you want to talk about it, Dee Dee?"

For just an instant I suspected him of mocking me, but it was Dee Dee he was looking at. She was so angry, her face was red.

"You and your cruel sense of humor!" she snapped. "I already told you what Sarah asked me about the house. You're a creep, Eric!"

I didn't understand what was disturbing her so much. If Eric wanted an answer, I'd give him one, but I'd hedge. I wished Dee Dee hadn't told him what I'd asked. "Mom loves this place," I answered. "I was just cleaning the maid's room, and we were talking about making it into a library."

Dee Dee jumped into the conversation as though she'd been reprieved. "A library! Don't tell me you like to read."

43

"I do like to read. A lot."

"That's great," she said. "I'd love to see what books you've got."

"You can help me unpack them," I told her, "and borrow any you like." Right now I didn't want to talk about books. I thought about the woman who had called to me in Spanish. It dawned on me that maybe I could get some information from Eric and Dee Dee. "Did anyone in the Holt family speak Spanish?" I asked.

Dee Dee gave a little start. "Adam probably learned some in school. We all did. Why in the world do you want to know that?"

"What about a Spanish-speaking maid? You lived right next door to the Holts. You'd know if they had a maid."

"A maid?" She shrugged. "I have no idea. I told you, the Holts kept to themselves. Let's talk about something else."

"If they had a maid, you'd see her going in and out, wouldn't you?"

"Not necessarily," she answered impatiently. "I suppose I would if the Holts had day help, someone who arrived in a car. But if they had live-in help—especially if she was an illegal alien, like Lupita, and didn't want to be noticed—that's a different matter. Mrs. Taylor, who lives on the corner, had a live-in maid for over a year before I knew she was there, and she wasn't here illegally. And I remember when—"

I interrupted her. In a way I was talking to myself, trying to sort through my own confusion. "Are you sure there wasn't someone in this house who spoke Spanish?"

Eric looked at me with an odd expression. "I think the Holts hired a couple of illegals on and off over the years, but as far as I know, they didn't have anyone working for them when—when they moved."

Dee Dee shrugged. "Eric would know if anyone would. He's probably the only one on the block who was ever invited inside the Holts' house, and that wasn't even very often, because Mrs. Holt didn't like Adam to get the house messed up, so Adam didn't have very many friends. In fact, Eric was probably his only real friend."

"Don't make it sound like it's over and done with. Adam and I are still friends," Eric snapped.

"Dad said that the Holts got divorced," I told them. "Does Adam live in Houston?"

Dee Dee shifted on the couch, but Eric said, "Adam had to live with his mother in California."

"Where in California?"

"It's a little town—Cedar Creek." He scowled. "What difference does it make?"

I leaned forward. "Tell me about the Holts. What were they like?"

Dee Dee twisted her fingers together. "The Holts are history. There's a lot more interesting stuff to talk about."

Eric studied my face. "Why are you asking so many questions, Sarah? And what's all this about someone speaking Spanish?"

There was no way I was going to tell them what had

happened to me in this house. I fumbled for an answer. "We're living in the Holts' house. It makes me curious. And Dee Dee's parents have a Spanish-speaking maid, so I just sort of wondered if the Holts had one too." I didn't sound convincing, not even to myself.

Dee Dee threw Eric a frantic look, as though she were asking for help. He ignored her, so she jumped to her feet and said, "I've really got to go. I'm supposed to baby-sit tonight, and I have to wash my hair and do a lot of stuff."

Maybe Eric could tell me what I wanted to know. "Eric, you don't have to go, do you?" The words came out so eagerly, I wished I could take them back. He was going to get the wrong idea. I felt myself blushing.

Dee Dee looked a little surprised, but Eric stood up and stretched, a smug expression on his face. "It's tough to disappoint you, Sarah, but I never date girls who are taller than I am," he said.

I couldn't help it. I laughed. For a few moments Eric glowered at me. "That was rude," I mumbled. "I'm sorry."

My apology didn't help. He was angry, so I was surprised when he said, "There *is* a guy you ought to meet, though. He's tall, and he likes tall girls. Yeah. The more I think about it, the better I like the idea. I think he would too."

Dee Dee looked at Eric sharply. "What's his name?"

"Anthony's his name, but we call him Tony. Tony Harris." Eric grinned and added, "You don't know him."

"Does he go to Memorial?"

"No, he doesn't, and it's none of your business, anyway. He wouldn't be interested in you."

"You're a conceited jerk," she said.

"And you're a nerd."

Trying to head off any more insults, I steered Dee Dee toward the door. "I wish you'd come over tomorrow morning," I told her. "Have you got a bike? Maybe we could go for a ride and you could show me around the neighborhood."

"Okay," Dee Dee said. "If you want to." She looked at me unhappily, as though there was a lot more on her mind she'd like to say but didn't know how.

Eric edged past us through the open door. "I'll get back to you about Tony," he told me. There was a mischievous, mocking look on his face that bothered me.

Dee Dee watched him walk out of earshot, then turned to me and said, "Sarah, I like you. I'd really like us to be friends. And it's not my fault. I mean, I hope you can understand, and it really doesn't matter because—"

I put a hand on her arm, interrupting her. "What are you talking about, Dee Dee?"

She looked down at the ground a moment, then up again, and her pale blue eyes stared into mine. "Don't mind the way I rattle on. Just promise me, please, that you'll stop talking about the Holts?"

"If it bothers you so much," I answered slowly.

"It bothers me a lot," she said. She backed away, moving toward the lawn. "See you tomorrow. Okay?"

I smiled at her. "Sure. Tomorrow." As I shut the door the house seemed to sigh as though glad the visitors had gone.

A few hours later Dad arrived home. His face was gray as he called Mom and me into the den. "Sit down," he said. "Please, sit down. I've got something to tell you."

"Your job!" Mom gasped as she slowly lowered herself into one of the chairs. "They just gave you a promotion. They wouldn't—"

Dad shook his head impatiently. "No, Dorothy. I haven't lost my job. It's something else, and it may or may not turn out to be a problem."

He tossed a quick, nervous look in my direction before he turned back to Mom.

"I feel as though we've been cheated. Legally, she was correct; but ethically, what she did was wrong. And the neighbors—not one of them gave me the facts. I resent that."

"Ron!" Mom said. "Make sense! What are you talking about?"

Dad took a deep breath. "I'm trying to make excuses for myself," he said. "I'll get to the point." He sat on the edge of the sofa next to me and leaned toward Mom. "Evelyn Pritchard didn't tell me the reason why this house hadn't sold, why it was priced so far below market value. I found out today when one of the secretaries in the office recognized our address."

Dad paused and glanced toward the entry hall as he added, "Just a little over two years ago a murder took place inside this house!"

48

Chapter
Four

Suddenly the vision of the blood on the tiles and the voice calling for help made sense. They were real. They had taken place in this house, and I had picked up on them. I'd seen the aftermath, but what about the murder itself? I shuddered and rubbed my arms, trying to warm them. Why was someone trying to involve me in this?

Mom's eyes sparked with anger, and her words were as clipped and sharp as if they were burning her tongue. "Evelyn Pritchard should have told you about the murder, Ron. Or one of the neighbors should have spoken up." She stood and paced to the door and back, then suddenly dropped into her chair again, her fingertips white as she gripped the chair arms. "Today I was very pointedly told that Evelyn is a wonderful friend and neighbor. The people on this block were shielding her, and that's not fair!"

"It was more than that," Dad explained, bitterness in

his voice. "The empty house hurt everyone's property values."

"I thought our neighbors were going to be nice people. I'd hoped they'd be friends." Mom reached over to take Dad's hand and asked, "Oh, Ron, what are we going to do?"

Dad sighed. "I've already spoken to an attorney. Legally, what Evelyn did was acceptable. All we can do is try to sell the house." He added, "If that's our decision."

"If?" Mom asked.

"We have to face facts, Dorothy. Look how long this house was on the market before we bought it. We can't afford to rent or buy another place to live in while we wait to see if someone wants to buy this. And when we tell them the situation . . ." He said quietly, "We'd have to. We couldn't do what Evelyn did."

"No," Mom said. "We couldn't." They both glanced toward me as though the thought had struck them at the same time.

"Sarah," Mom said, "something about the house frightened you when you first set foot in it. What was it? You didn't—" She took a deep breath, steadying herself. "That strange feeling didn't come back, did it?"

"No, it didn't. It's never coming back." What else could I tell them? Dad had just pointed out that we couldn't afford to make two monthly house payments. They were both watching me, waiting for more of an answer, so I tried to choose my words carefully and said, "Didn't you ever walk in on two people who'd just had an argument? You can feel the tension in the air. That's the best way to explain what I felt."

50

Mom's expression was so dubious that I smiled and added, "Remember when we went to visit your cousin Linda and her husband? You said later you knew the minute you set foot in their house that they'd been having a terrible argument. You told us you could feel it in the air."

"That was different," Mom said.

I just smiled again and shrugged. That desperate cry for help still gripped me, and I ached for the poor terrified woman. I had said I would help her, and I keep my promises, so there was nothing more I could tell my parents.

"Mom turned to Dad. "Are you sure there isn't some way to get out of this contract?"

"I'm positive." Dad let out an unhappy sigh. "I made a stupid mistake in buying this house," he said. "I was feeling so proud of myself, so glad to get such a bargain. I should have questioned why the house was so much below market value."

Both Mom and Dad looked so miserable that I felt guilty. If they weren't so worried about me . . . I tried to sound as matter-of-fact as I could, and said, "People don't tear down houses just because someone's been murdered in them. Other people buy those houses and live in them."

They stared at me, surprised, and I went on. "This is the nicest house we've ever lived in. Let's enjoy it. The murder is over and done with. Mom, you didn't feel anything unusual in this house. Neither did Dad. It didn't bother you before you learned about the murder, so why get upset about it now?"

"Well . . ." Mom hesitated. "It's just knowing that . . ."

"Sarah is probably right," Dad said. He actually began to look hopeful.

Mom glanced at the windows. "Maybe we should have burglar bars installed on all the windows. If it was someone on drugs who broke in, looking for something to steal, it could happen again."

"It wasn't like that." Dad shook his head.

"What did happen?" I asked Dad. "The people who told you about the murder must have given you the whole story."

"Are you sure you want to know?" Dad's face sagged. He looked terrible.

"Yes," I answered. "We're going to hear it sooner or later. We'd rather hear it from you."

Dad glanced at Mom for confirmation, and she gave a slight nod, so he said, "I remember reading something about the murder in our Missouri newspaper, but at the time I didn't pay much attention, so when I arranged to buy the house, the address and the name Holt didn't mean anything."

"You met the Holts when you signed the papers for the house, didn't you?" Mom asked.

"I met the father of the family—Martin Holt. He was a pleasant enough fellow, but his name still meant nothing to me."

"Was it his wife who was murdered?" Mom whispered. "Or his son?"

"Neither." Dad took a deep breath and continued. "A woman who lives on Fair Oaks Drive called a nearby

Pizza Express and ordered a pizza. It was around one o'clock in the afternoon. She called a couple of times later complaining that her order hadn't been delivered. The girl who had been hired to deliver pizzas hadn't come back to the restaurant for the next order, so around two-thirty the manager went looking for her. The boy who had taken the phone order had scribbled something on the order blank that looked like Fair Oaks Lane, instead of Drive."

"Fair Oaks Lane. Our street," Mom said.

Dad continued, his voice flat with the horror of what he had to tell. "The manager found the Pizza Express delivery car parked about a block away on a side street. There was no sign of the girl, so he called the police. During their investigation they went to this address on Fair Oaks Lane. No one was home, but the side door to our garage—*the* garage—was standing open, and they could see a crumpled box from Pizza Express. On the garage floor, tossed next to the trash can, were a rag with stains that looked like blood and a pair of bloodstained tennis shoes."

Mom shuddered, hugging her arms and rubbing them as though she were cold. "Don't mind me," she said as Dad paused. "Go on."

"The police on the scene called in for a search warrant," Dad told us, "and in the meantime some other police officers and a film crew from a television station arrived. Some of the neighbors who were home came out to see what was going on. At this point Adam Holt— the teenage son—drove into the street, saw the cars and people at his house, and did a U-turn, trying to get away.

But a neighbor had seen him and pointed him out, so the police chased him for a few blocks and caught him.

"Adam Holt confessed to murdering the girl and told the police he had buried her body in a nearby woods. It was getting dark by this time, too late to search, so the police took him downtown and booked him."

"Thank goodness they caught him," Mom said.

"That's not quite all of it," Dad said. "When the detectives arrived at the Holt house with a search warrant, they discovered that the parents had arrived home. In fact, they'd been home for about twenty minutes. Their son had attempted to clean up some of the blood but hadn't done a very good job of it, so they'd seen—"

"The blood on the walls and floor of the entry hall," I said, interrupting.

"Yes, and some stains on the stairway carpet that hadn't come out." Dad stopped and looked at me with a puzzled expression. "How did you know about the blood?"

"Uh—it figures. Go on," I answered quickly. "Tell us the rest."

He did. "Although the parents had found their son missing and the bloodstains in the entry hall, they hadn't called the police. When they were informed about what had happened, Mr. Holt immediately hired an attorney for his son."

"How old was Adam Holt?" I asked.

"Only seventeen," Dad said.

"Why did he kill the girl?"

"Apparently, from what he first told the police, he

54

tried to force her into the house. She fought back, so he stabbed her."

"That's horrible! I hope he got life imprisonment."

"He's not in prison," Dad said. "His attorney kept him from making a written or taped confession, and an oral confession that hasn't been tape-recorded or witnessed by someone other than a police officer isn't admissible as evidence in the state of Texas. When Adam Holt came to trial, the judge allowed the oral confession as evidence, in spite of the law, and the jury convicted Adam of murder in the first degree. The defense attorney appealed, and the conviction was thrown out by a higher court."

"But the blood! The pizza box in his garage! Wouldn't that be enough evidence?" Mom asked.

"No. Apparently not. There was no one to place him at the scene of the crime. Adam Holt was never put on the witness stand. His defense had been that he had been ill with the flu, was having an allergic reaction to his medication, and didn't know what he was doing or even where he was at the time. Without an eyewitness to place Adam at the scene of the crime, the district attorney couldn't make a strong enough case."

"That's crazy!"

"But that's Texas law," Dad said. "I was told it's the only state that won't allow an unrecorded oral confession as evidence."

"You didn't tell us if they found the girl's body," I said.

"They did, but not in the general area the Holt boy had indicated. It was on the opposite side of Houston. A gas-station attendant happened to be watching the ten-o'clock news, saw Adam's picture, and remembered filling the tank of his car earlier in the day, so he called the police. The gas station was near a rarely used, unpaved road that was muddy from recent rains. Adam's car was caked with mud, so the attendant knew he'd been back in the woods. Early the next morning, as soon as it was light, the police checked the area the attendant had described and found the murdered girl's body there."

"I should think that would be enough evidence against him!" Mom insisted.

"I guess it wasn't strong enough to warrant another trial. It was still only circumstantial."

"It's so different on those television shows," Mom said. "They're always trying the wrong person, but the attorney holds up something like a matchbook cover or a piece of an earring and says to the guilty person, 'This means you were the real murderer!' and they arrest the guilty one and let the innocent one go."

"It's a lot more complicated than that in real life," Dad told her.

"There's something weird about the story you told us," I said to Dad. "Why would Adam confess to the crime and then lie about where he'd put the body?"

"Some people get so mixed up in lies, they're unable to differentiate between lies and truth," Dad explained.

"It's the parents I don't understand," Mom said. "If I came home and found my child missing, and blood on the walls and floor, the first thing I'd do would be to call the police."

She looked at me as though to prove I were still here

in one piece, and added, "I can't help worrying about the effect this house might have on Sarah."

I tried a laugh, and it came out a little shaky. "Remember that old-fashioned hotel in Colorado where we vacationed two summers ago? The manager told us about the shoot-outs and murders that had taken place in their lobby and saloon back in the days of the Wild West. We just thought of it as an interesting part of history, and it didn't bother our sleep. Right?"

"Sweetheart, that was different."

"Not really, Mom. Those ranch hands—even the gunslingers—were real people. They didn't want to die, either."

Mom persisted. "It's different because *you're* different. When we stayed at that hotel, it was before—well—before you began having those hallucinations."

I got up and walked to the window. The sun's heat was shimmering in waves from the street and sidewalk, but the house was cold. Much too cold. "The presence that followed me is gone, Mom. I told you that."

"Well . . ." Mom hesitated.

"Dorothy, listen to Sarah. Whatever happened here is over and done with," Dad said. His voice was firm again, and color had come back into his face, but his voice dropped as he added, "I honestly don't see what other choice we can make for the moment."

Mom thought a moment, then said, "I want to do whatever is best for Sarah, but I don't know what that is. All we can do is leave the decision up to her."

The air shifted. I found myself in a different time and place. I took a deep breath, inhaling a pungent scent of

57

cloves from the kitchen and stale tobacco smoke from the drapes. As deep shadows stretched like spread fingers across the thick and ragged lawn below the window, I began to feel the quiet presence of the woman. Although I couldn't see her, I recognized the warm, spicy-sour scent of her skin. Her voice spoke within my head, begging me, frantically pleading, *¡Ayúdame! ¡Por favor!*

Who are you? I didn't speak the words. I thought them.

The answer came, but I didn't understand.

I don't know what you're saying. You'll have to help me.

A word, hoarse with tears, slid into my mind. *Muerte.*

Muerte? I knew that word. Death. I gasped as the realization struck me. *Are you the one who was murdered here?*

The tears were so real that I could feel them damp against my cheek. *Ayúdame,* she whispered.

"Sarah?" Mom asked. "Did you hear me? Is something the matter?"

I closed my eyes, willing myself back to the present. When I opened them, the room was normal, but the voice lingered in my mind.

"What is it?"

"I—I got dizzy for a minute. I'm all right now," I told her. I was afraid of the woman who spoke to me, yet at the same time, by agreeing to help her and become a link between this woman's world and mine, I had a strange yearning to see her, to reassure her. She had reached out to me, and I couldn't turn away from her cry for help.

"Are you sure you're all right?" Mom asked.

"Positive."

Dad sat forward on the edge of the sofa. "We need your decision, Sarah. It's important to us."

"I want to live here, in this house," I answered. The air that riffled against my cheek was like the soft touch of a warm hand.

"Then as far as I'm concerned, it's decided. We'll stay," Mom told Dad.

He leaned against the back of the sofa and gave a sigh of relief.

We all jumped at the ring of the telephone. "I'll answer," I said.

"Hey, Sarah," Eric said, "I talked to that guy about you."

"What guy?" I was still so deeply into what Dad had told us that I didn't know what Eric was talking about.

"Tony Harris. Remember? The tall guy who likes tall girls." A strange tone came into Eric's voice, as though he were secretly laughing at me. "Tony wants to meet you."

"I—I don't think so," I told him. I was uncomfortable with Eric. "We've just moved in. I want to get used to Houston first. I'm not ready to start dating yet."

Mom, who had picked up a magazine, pretending to read it, was suddenly alert. She motioned to me, smiling and mouthing, "Who is it?"

"Are you there?" Eric asked. "Did you hear what I said?"

"I'm sorry," I answered, deliberately turning my

back on Mom. "My mother was trying to tell me something, so I was distracted. What did you say?"

"I said, if you haven't had dinner yet, Tony knows this great Mexican restaurant, and he could meet us there."

"Why can't Tony come here?"

"The restaurant's in West University. It would be kind of crazy if he drove all the way here to pick you up, then drove all the way back, wouldn't it?"

I was on firm ground now. "My parents won't let me date someone they haven't met."

"It isn't really a date," Eric said. "Anyhow, I'll be with you. I'll come over and meet them." His voice became mocking again. "They can even meet my parents if they're so protective of their darling daughter."

My face grew hot. I didn't know if I was blushing because I was embarrassed or angry. "Forget it!" I snapped.

It was Eric's turn to be embarrassed. "Hey, I'm sorry," he said. "That's just my brand of humor. Dee Dee says it's cruel. Maybe she's right. I should have realized you aren't used to it yet. I was just trying to be funny."

"It wasn't funny."

"I'll come over right now," Eric said. "I was so sure you'd want to meet Tony that I set up the plan. Tony was going out to run some errands, so I can't call him back. He'll be waiting in the restaurant for us. Please say you'll come, Sarah. Okay?"

Grudgingly I agreed, "Well, all right. Come on over."

"Great!" he said. "I'll be there in five minutes." And he slammed down the receiver.

60

Whispers from the Dead

I turned to Mom and said, before she could ask, "That was Eric Hendrickson. He wants to take me to dinner at a Mexican restaurant in West University so I can meet a friend of his who wants to meet me."

Mom was dubious. "Eric—the boy who asked for a beer."

Dad looked puzzled, so she explained.

"He was probably showing off a little, because he's two years older than Sarah," Dad said, and smiled. "I remember what being eighteen was like."

The doorbell rang, and I ran to answer, leading Eric into the den. He was polite and friendly, and I could see Mom melt.

"I'll take very good care of Sarah and make sure she's home early," Eric said with such sincerity, it made me want to gag.

Mom beamed at him and said to me, "If you'd like to go with Eric to meet his friend, Tony, we have no objections. You need to make friends in Houston, Sarah."

I couldn't think of a good reason to refuse, so I excused myself to put on a skirt and blouse. I picked up my hairbrush, then put it down again, slowly turning from my bedroom mirror to face the room. The air was trembling against the back of my neck.

I groaned and murmured, "Don't do this to me! Not now! Go away!" Groping for the little Spanish I remembered from lessons in elementary school, I found the word and said, *"¡Váyase!"*

The silence that followed was as taut as a held breath. Feeling a little guilty, I waited. Finally I whispered, "I don't know what you want yet, but I'll try to find out. I promise to help you, but you can't keep pestering me. Okay?"

There was no answer, only the icy tickle of someone else's fear.

Chapter Five

Sarah! What's keeping you?" Eric called from the foot of the stairs. The tension in my room shattered.

"Coming!" I yelled. I brushed back my hair, snatched up my shoulder bag, and ran down the stairs.

Eric drove a white BMW. He told me about his car in great detail while I made appropriate murmurs and wished we could talk about something more interesting. Then, abruptly, he asked, "Why did you tell Dee Dee that the Holt house scares you?"

"I said the house was weird, that's all."

"The word Dee Dee used was *scared.*" He quickly turned to look at me, his eyes crinkling at the corners as though he were enjoying a secret laugh at my expense, before he faced the road again. "You'll find out sooner or later that Dee Dee is a mouth. If you tell her anything, she spills it."

"Come off it," I muttered. "There's no secret to enjoy at my expense any longer. We know about the murder."

The car swerved slightly, and the driver in the car in the next lane leaned on his horn.

Before Eric could answer, I said, "It was bad enough for Dee Dee's mother not to tell Dad about the murder, but what about the rest of you? Why didn't your parents tell him the truth before he bought the house?"

He looked embarrassed. "What were we supposed to do, put a sign in the front yard? 'A murder took place in this house'? Frankly we were all glad when the house was sold."

"Would *you* like to live in a house where a murder took place?"

Eric shrugged. "It wouldn't bother me. What's the big deal? You don't believe in ghosts, do you?"

"Let's talk about something else," I said. "Tell me about the high school."

He did, and it filled the time until we arrived at the restaurant.

Tony Harris was waiting for us just inside the door. As we entered, standing under a bright pool of light from a multicolored glass chandelier, he stepped from the shadows and smiled. He didn't even glance at Eric. His eyes, a vibrant blue, locked into mine, and I caught my breath.

Tony seemed older than Eric. He was tall, about two inches taller than I am. He was broad-shouldered but slender, and his hair and mustache were dark brown. "Hello, Sarah," he said in a voice as soft as dark silk.

Infatuation. I had heard the word. Suddenly I knew what it meant, how exciting it could be.

64

Whispers from the Dead

I moved a little closer to him, unable to look away, mesmerized by his voice and his eyes. Tony wasn't that handsome. He was really kind of average-looking, but there was something different, something exciting, behind his smile; and something so demanding in his look that shivers ran up my spine. He reached out and took my hand, and I grasped his fingers willingly.

"Come on, old buddy," Eric said, and slapped Tony on the shoulder. "I'm starving. You and Sarah can get acquainted while we eat."

Tony, still holding my hand, turned to follow the restaurant's hostess, but the spell hadn't broken. I was drawn to Tony, hungry to look back into his eyes. The sensation startled me. I'd never felt like this about anyone before. Andy? No. I could hardly remember Andy's face.

We were ushered into a booth. Eric pushed me in first, then slid in next to me. Tony sat across from me. As we ate and talked, Eric proudly told us about some of the practical jokes he'd played on unsuspecting friends— especially the mean, embarrassing practical jokes. I disliked Eric even more and wished he'd be quiet. I wasn't interested in him. I was interested in Tony. But while Eric was talking, he had Tony's attention, and that gave me a chance to study Tony without his noticing it. I liked his smile and the way he lifted back his head when he laughed.

Tony had a quiet nature. He was somewhat of a loner, he told me, when Eric finally gave him a chance, and we talked about books. We both liked biographies and mysteries. I was surprised that our tastes were so much alike

65

and felt even more drawn toward Tony. I was eager to learn all about him.

As he reached across the table for the bowl of salsa, the sleeve of his long-sleeved sport shirt pulled back from his wrist and I noticed an irregular purple mark the size of a quarter.

Tony turned, caught my glance at his wrist, and tugged down the cuff of his sleeve. It surprised me. I didn't think he would be the type to be self-conscious about a birthmark. Lots of people have them.

Eric suddenly gulped down what was left of his iced tea and looked at me with such a wicked smile, I was startled.

"What's the matter with you?" I began, but Eric quickly turned away and squeezed out of the booth.

"I've got some errands to run," he said.

Reluctantly I gathered up my shoulder bag and started to follow him, but Tony reached across the booth, his fingers closing firmly on my arm. "Don't go," he said. "I'll take you home."

"Good idea. Why don't you do that?" Eric said. His face was serious, but that strange smile had moved into his eyes. Was he planning another practical joke? At my expense? I didn't know how to protect myself against him.

Eric turned and said to me, "There's a guy I've got to see. It will work out a lot better for me if Tony gives you a ride home."

"You told Mom—" I began, but Eric was already half-way to the restaurant door. Flustered, I stammered to Tony, "I—I'm supposed to b-be home early." My breath caught in my throat, and I felt a little scared, maybe because of the feelings I had for Tony. I didn't understand them. I knew very little about him, but when he smiled at me, nothing else seemed to matter.

The waitress flew past, slapping the check on the table. Tony pulled out his wallet and paid the bill. He edged out of the booth, unfolding his long legs, and reached out a hand to me. "I'll take you home now," he said.

His black sports car, with its dark-tinted glass, had a clean, fresh, new-car smell, and the dashboard gleamed. He fussed with the car, adjusting the rearview mirrors, checking the digital clock light, and fiddling with the radio until he found a station he liked. He kept the music low as he drove north on Kirby. "Have you seen much of Houston?" he asked.

"Hardly any of it," I answered.

Tony turned to me and smiled. "We can take care of that."

I could feel myself melting into his smile, so I struggled to stay clearheaded, saying the first thing that came into my mind. "Tell me about yourself. Where did you meet Eric?"

"We used to be in school together."

"But you're older than he is."

"Not much more than a year." He grinned. "It's the mustache that gives me that older, distinguished look."

I laughed with him. "Are you in college?"

"Not right now. I've been busy with other things. I might go East to school. I haven't made up my mind yet."

67

"Do you know what you want to study?"

"I've been thinking about pre-law. I might like to be a lawyer." As we turned left onto a tree-lined street named San Felipe, Tony reached over and took my hand. I could feel the warmth spread all the way through my body. I was glad it was so dark that Tony couldn't see the flush on my cheeks.

"Enough questions from you," Tony said. "It's my turn to ask a few. "Eric told me that you were frightened by something in your house. What was it?"

I glanced at him quickly, but he looked straight ahead, waiting for my answer. I wasn't about to tell him. I remembered too well the expressions on the faces of my friends when I'd been open with them about the spirit that had shadowed me. "It—it wasn't really anything," I managed to tell Tony. "It was just a—well, a feeling I had when I entered the house for the first time."

"What kind of feeling?"

"I don't know how to describe it."

We stopped for a red light and Tony turned toward me, his eyes drilling into mine. "Try."

I shivered, and Tony immediately began adjusting the vents for the air conditioner. "I'm sorry," he said. "You've been getting the full blast. Is that better?"

"Yes." I paused. "I don't know what you want me to tell you or why."

His smile was easy. We were back in traffic, and his attention was on the road. "Just curious," he said. "Your reaction to the house—according to what Dee Dee told Eric—was unusual, to say the least."

"I never should have talked about it to Dee Dee. She blew it all out of proportion."

"Do you know what happened in that house?"

"Yes. The murder." I shivered again, and this time it was not because of the air conditioner. "Why don't we talk about something else?" A short time before, I'd been trying to get more information about the Holts. But I didn't want it now. Not from Tony.

"Don't you think the story of the murder is interesting?"

"Interesting? No! I don't want to think about it at all!"

"We knew Adam. Did Eric tell you?"

"Yes. Eric says that he and Adam are still friends."

"That's because Eric believed Adam's claim that he was having a reaction to his medication and didn't know what he was doing. Not everyone bought that excuse."

I glanced at him sharply. "Do you believe Adam?"

"There's no reason why I shouldn't."

I was becoming very uncomfortable with this conversation. "I don't want to talk about Adam Holt," I told Tony.

He looked at me sharply, then turned away. I couldn't catch the expression on his face. "According to Eric, you had a lot of questions to ask."

"I know, but—"

"Like wondering who in the household spoke Spanish. That's a strange question. Why did you want to know?"

"Does it matter?"

"No. It just seemed like an unusual thing for you to ask. If there's something about the house that bothers

69

you and you want to talk about it, I won't put you off the way Eric and Dee Dee did. I'll listen. I'll listen to anything you'd like to tell me, Sarah."

Tony's voice was deep and soothing, and I began to relax. But I was determined not to tell Tony what I had heard and seen. Strange Sarah. I couldn't let Tony think that of me.

"Thanks," I told him, trying to keep my voice light, "but there really isn't anything to tell. Let's talk about something else—anything at all."

"Anything at all?" Tony's eyes sparked with the kind of wicked gleam I'd seen in Eric's. "Okay. There's something else I'd like to talk about." His fingers tightened on mine, and his thumb stroked the back of my hand. "Have you ever been in love, Sarah?"

Again he'd caught me off-balance. My hand tingled, and it was hard to breathe. "N-no," I said, stuttering. "Not really."

"A beautiful girl like you? That's hard to believe." We came to another stoplight and he turned to smile at me. "Have you ever wondered what it would be like?"

I leaned a little closer to him, as though my body were behaving independently of my mind, as though Tony and I were magnets being drawn together. The way I was reacting frightened me. I inched back against the seat and said, as firmly as I could, "Tony, I just met you. I've only known you for a couple of hours."

"A lot can happen in a couple of hours, Sarah." His voice was low, the way it was when he first said my name. Again shivers ran up and down my backbone.

"Please, Tony, take it easy."

70

Whispers from the Dead

I was surprised to see him make a left turn into the driveway of our house. I hadn't been paying attention to the route. I didn't know we were so close to home.

I pulled my hand away from his. "Why don't you come in and meet my mom and dad?"

"I'd like that," Tony said. "But we'll have to plan introductions for the next time. I'm supposed to pick up my own mom at nine-thirty." He glanced at the digital clock on the dashboard. "I'm going to be late as it is."

"They'll ask about you, since you brought me home instead of Eric."

Tony reached over and lightly ran one fingertip down the side of my face, resting it for just an instant on my lips. I trembled and sucked in my breath. His eyes were so demanding, so intense. He leaned back and smiled at me. "I'll meet them next time, Sarah," he said.

Obviously he was waiting for me to get out of the car. He must have been unaware of the effect he was having on me, and I was thankful. I didn't understand the peculiar sensations in my body, or how to control them. "T-thanks for dinner. I—I liked the restaurant," I said, still stammering. I was reluctant to see him go, and angry with myself for feeling that way.

As I walked toward the front door Tony lowered the window on the driver's side and said, "I'll call you soon. I got your telephone number from Eric."

I gave a quick wave of the hand as I turned and hurried to unlock the front door. I desperately wanted him to call me, and I was afraid it must show in my eyes. My face still tingled where his fingertip had touched it.

Alone, in the entry hall, I heard the whispery noises

again, and little scuttling sounds seemed to scurry throughout the house. Beside me the stairway creaked, and I ran to join Mom and Dad.

Of course they had questions about Tony. I knew they would.

Mom flipped off the television set and slipped her shoes back on. "He could have come in for just a few minutes," she complained.

"Tony had to pick up his mother, and he was late."

"We like to know who you're going out with," Mom continued. "Eric had promised he'd take you home."

I was uncomfortable with the disapproval in her voice. I wanted her to like Tony. "You'll meet Tony soon," I told her. "He said he'd call me. And you'll like him. He's—well, he's wonderful." I couldn't help blushing, and—to my relief—Mom laughed.

"When I was your age," she said, "I had the most awful crush on a boy in my class. I blushed every time he looked in my direction."

This wasn't a crush. The feeling I had for Tony was very different. It was exciting and wonderful and scary all at the same time. I didn't want to tell Mom that. I just wanted to hug it to myself, not sharing it with anyone.

"This has been an exhausting day," Dad said. He stood and stretched. "I'm ready for bed."

Mom said, "It takes a while, doesn't it, to get used to new places and new ways." She put an arm around his waist and rested her head against his. "Do you miss the Missouri office?"

There was such wistfulness in her voice that he hugged her shoulders tightly. "In any move there's bound to be a few new ways to get used to, but everyone in the department's been friendly. Well, almost everyone." He smiled. "I suppose there's at least one stumbling block in every office—maybe to keep life from getting too routine." He paused before he asked, "Did I ask too much? Is this move too hard on you, Dorothy?"

"I've shed a few tears," Mom said. She straightened and smiled at Dad. "But I'm a survivor. As soon as the house is put together, I'll go job-hunting. As for tomorrow, I'm going to start hanging pictures." She headed toward the kitchen, saying as she'd done for years, "I'll check to see if the doors are locked."

Dad turned off the reading lamp next to his chair and walked toward the hall. He stopped and waited for me. "Coming, Sarah?"

I realized that ever since I'd walked into the house I'd been waiting for another contact from the woman. A question suddenly popped into my mind. "Dad," I asked, "that woman who was murdered—what was her name?"

He sighed. "I don't think we should get into that again."

"I'm not going to talk about it," I said. "I only want to know the woman's name."

He frowned, trying to remember. "It was Darlene. Darlene what? Let's see . . . Garwood? No. That's close, but it was something else, more rhythmic. Garwood, Garlin. That's it—Darlene Garland."

"Are you sure? That name doesn't fit someone who only spoke Spanish."

"I don't know where you got the idea that she only spoke Spanish. She would have had to speak English to

73

hold the kind of job she had—especially in this neighborhood, where most of the people speak English."

Dad looked at me with a kind of funny expression on his face, so I quickly said, "I guess I was confused. There was so much to think about."

"Yes," he said. "There was." He put an arm around my shoulder and kissed my forehead. "I'm proud of you, Sarah. If you'd been afraid to live in this house, I don't know what we would have done. You even managed to reassure your mother with your sensible, practical attitude, and that took some doing."

I hugged him tightly, wishing I could tell him about the vision and the woman who had asked me for help. But I couldn't. I wished we could be back in Missouri, but that was a stupid wish that wouldn't come true.

Mom returned and kissed me good night. I left them and took the stairs one slow step at a time, trying to sort everything out.

Who was the woman who had contacted me? Was she someone who really needed my help? Or had the evil in this house twisted itself into demons who pretended to be what they were not? Nervously I turned on the light switch in my room before I turned off the light in the hall.

With trembling fingers I closed my bedroom door and leaned against it, waiting for—no, actually *willing*—the voice to return.

Chapter Six

The spirit chose her own moments to make contact. When I realized she wouldn't come, I was free to think about Tony, who slipped from my conscious thoughts into my dreams.

I woke to slotted ribbons of sunlight streaming through the mini-blinds and to a whisper: *"Trate de encontrarlo."*

I sat up in bed, swinging my feet to the floor, and brushing my hair away from my face. *"Trate de encontrarlo"*? I said out loud. "What does that mean?" Had the words come from my dream?

If I'd moved, I would have missed the slight hiss of a breath taken and held. Hugging my arms to keep from shivering, I whispered, "Are you there?"

No one answered.

Anxious to escape whoever was with me, I rummaged through my shoulder bag to find a scrap of paper and a pen and wrote down the words so I wouldn't forget them.

It didn't take long to pull on shorts and a T-shirt and race downstairs to join Mom in the kitchen where she was still rearranging pans in the lower cabinets.

She looked up at me in surprise. "You're out of breath," she said.

"Hungry, I guess," I answered, and kissed the top of her head.

"Help yourself to some cereal," she told me. "The bowls are now in the cupboard on the far right."

As I poured milk over my cereal I asked, "Mom, have we got a Spanish-English phrase book?"

She looked up, surprised. "No. Why do you want one?"

Hunching over my cereal, I mumbled, "There are some things I want to look up. I need to brush up on my Spanish."

"There are a number of bookstores near here," she said. "Two on Memorial, not too far. Why don't you buy one?"

"I think I will." I waited until she was through rattling pans and asked, "What can I do to help you?"

"Nothing for the next few hours," Mom said. "I want to get a little better organized first, then I'll have lots for you to do."

It was too early for the bookstores to be open, and I wanted to get away from the house—and the voice that haunted me. "I'm going to go for a quick bike ride," I told Mom. "I'll be back in about fifteen or twenty minutes."

The sun was already hot, and as I wheeled my bike from the garage I felt as though I'd stepped from a hot shower into a room filled with steam. Moisture clung to my skin, and the hair at the back of my neck curled into damp ringlets.

"Wait up!"

Dee Dee ran barefoot across the lawn to the street. I pulled over to the curb, bracing one foot against it, and said, "You're up early."

She grinned. She was wearing a faded, ripped, over-size T-shirt with a purple dinosaur on it that she'd slept in, I guessed. Her hair was still tousled, and her face was scrubbed clean, making her look like a mischievous twelve-year-old. "I'm always up early. How was your date last night? Was he cute? I want to hear all about him."

"The communication on this street is unbelievable," I answered.

She giggled. "I was curious. I wanted to find out about this guy Eric told you about. I've never heard Eric even mention him, so I called Eric, and he just happened to tell me he fixed the two of you up with a date. So . . . what was Tony like? Was he cute? What did you talk about?"

I stared right into Dee Dee's eyes without smiling. "We talked about the murder," I said.

Dee Dee gasped, and tears filled her eyes. "Oh, damn!" she said. "You're never going to want to speak to me again, are you?"

I got off my bike and laid it against the curb. "I'd like

us to be friends, but right now I'm awfully mad at your mother."

"I guess I don't blame you," Dee Dee said. "But her job is selling houses. What was she going to do?"

"She should have been honest and told my father about the murder."

"Then he wouldn't have bought the house. No one would." She glanced over her shoulder at our house and shivered. "It would have just sat there and crumbled. After the Holts moved out, somebody threw rocks into the front windows, and one night someone kicked in the back door. Nobody on the street wanted the house empty. Look at it our way. Don't you understand?"

"No," I said.

Dee Dee turned slowly and began to walk back to her house, so I added, "But I do want to be friends."

She lifted her head and smiled hopefully. "It would be awful living next door to you if you hated me."

I managed to smile back. "I doubt if anyone could hate you."

"Eric does—sometimes," she answered. "Of course, Eric hates almost everybody. He can be so mean when he feels like it." She wiggled her shoulders, as though she were tossing off the problem between us. "About Tony," she said. "I know he's tall, but what does he look like?"

"Nothing special, just okay," I answered, but I felt myself blush. Dee Dee grinned, but before she could say a word, I went on. "He's tall—just as Eric said—and he has a good tan, and his hair and mustache are dark brown."

78

"Mustache?" Her eyebrows rose. "How old is he?"

"He said he was a year older than Eric. That would make him nineteen."

"And you like him," Dee Dee said. It wasn't a question.

"Yes. I guess I do." I could feel my cheeks grow even warmer.

"Have you eaten breakfast?" Dee Dee asked. "I haven't. Come on in. I'll get Lupita to fix us something, and you can tell me all about Tony."

I didn't want to tell Dee Dee about Tony. I wanted to keep him to myself. I pointedly glanced at my watch, not really seeing it, and said, "I've got to get home. I told Mom I'd take a quick ride, then get back and help with the unpacking. I'll see you later."

"I could come over and help, too, if you'd like me to." She glanced at our house again from the corner of her eye. "Sooner or later I'll have to get used to being in the house."

"Just like we'll have to get used to *living* in it."

Dee Dee flinched.

I hadn't meant to hurt her. "I'm sorry," I told her. "All of this wasn't your fault."

Dee Dee blinked a couple of times, managed a smile, and said, "I'll be over in about an hour. Okay?"

"Great," I answered. "We'll put you to work."

When I finished my bike ride, I wheeled the bike into the garage and went back inside the house, where Mom was on her hands and knees, her head inside one of the kitchen cupboards.

"Are you sure I can't do that for you?" I asked.

79

She squirmed backward until she could sit upright. "No thanks," she said. "I know exactly where I want to put everything in my kitchen." She pointed toward the end of the counter. "I've made a shopping list. Why don't you take the car and run down to the store? By the time you've bought the groceries, the bookstores will be open. Then you can stop by the vet's and get Dinky."

"Good! I can't wait to see Dinky."

Mom tilted her head and examined me. "Why this interest in Spanish all of a sudden?"

"Lots of people in Houston speak Spanish." We'd always been open and honest with each other, so I felt uncomfortable about hiding my reason from her.

Mom sighed and said, "I know this move has been tough on you, Sarah, but when school starts, you'll make some friends."

"I have one friend here already—Dee Dee Pritchard." Mom's eyes clouded for an instant. Before she could say anything, I quickly added, "Dee Dee's nice. Really. Don't blame her for what her mother did."

"I know you're right," Mom said, although she didn't look very happy about it. "I'm still having trouble accepting what happened."

"Everything's going to be okay, Mom." I picked up the shopping list and hurried from the room. She'd always been good at reading my face.

While I was standing in line at the bookstore, waiting to buy a Spanish-English phrase book, I looked up the section on familiar phrases. *Lo necesito esta noche*—I need it tonight. *Aqui tiene la lista*—Here is the list. *Trate de encontrarlo*—Try to find it.

80

Try to find it! With trembling fingers I fumbled through my shoulder bag, pulled out the scrap of paper on which I'd written the words from my dream, and read them: *Trate de encontrarlo.* The same words. Try to find it. Try to find what?

"May I help you?" the clerk asked.

Quickly I paid for the book and hurried out to the car. I thumbed through the book, trying to find what I wanted to ask, but the verb to find, *encontrar,* was not conjugated. Here was *qué,* meaning "what." Could I combine them? Or just answer *"¿Qué?"* to whoever was trying to reach me?

When I picked up Dinky, I was so glad to have her in my arms again that I snuggled against her fur. She looked at me as though she blamed me for her visit at the vet's.

"It's not my fault," I told her, and tucked her inside the cat carrier. "Moving's been hard on all of us. Why should you be an exception?"

Dinky just sneered and turned her back to me.

Dee Dee arrived at my house just as I pulled into the driveway. "I'm ready to work," she said, and tugged one of the large grocery bags from the car. Spying the cat carrier, she said, "Hey! She's pretty."

Dinky looked at Dee Dee with a little more friendliness than she'd shown me, but once inside the house, Dinky went exploring, ignoring both of us. I watched her carefully to see how she reacted. Weren't cats supposed to sense things people couldn't see? But not a hair raised on Dinky's calico back.

81

Mom and Dee Dee greeted each other a little awkwardly.

"I'll put away the groceries," Mom said. She nodded toward the maid's room. "I'd appreciate it if you girls would do a really good job of wiping down the floor in there—especially in the little closet. It's a hands-and-knees job, and my back is beginning to give out."

Dee Dee and I equipped ourselves with soft old towels and the wood cleanser. "I'll begin in the closet," I said.

The closet was so small that I couldn't get completely into it. I attacked the baseboards, scrubbing hard. I was so intent on my work that at first I didn't notice that the air had changed. It grew warmer, and it touched my face in rhythm, as though someone were breathing.

I heard the words in my head. *Trate de encontrarlo.*

¿Qué? I demanded. *¿Qué, qué, qué?*

There was no answer, but the breathing became more rapid. *How can I help you if you don't tell me what you want?* I asked. Stubbornly I scrubbed even harder at the baseboard, working faster, trying to break the rhythm that surged against me. It was like an excited heartbeat, a gasping, a trembling, and it wouldn't leave me alone.

Suddenly a piece of the baseboard came away in my hands. "Oh, no!" I said. "I think I broke something." But I realized that I hadn't broken it. The board must have been loose. It pulled away too quickly.

The breathing stopped.

"What did you break?" Dee Dee was right beside me, peering over my shoulder.

82

I picked up the small piece of board—about eight or ten inches in length—to see if there were nails I might drive in a little deeper in order to fasten it in place, and I glimpsed a shallow, hollowed-out place, a rough gap in the Sheetrock. Inside this hollow was a bundle of papers with a thin silver chain wound around them.

"Move back, Dee Dee. I'm coming out." I squirmed backward into the room.

She plopped down beside me as I sat cross-legged on the floor, examining the small packet in my hands.

"What is it? Where did you find it?" she asked.

"It was tucked behind a loose piece of baseboard."

"That's a religious medal!" she said as I unwound the chain and exposed a round, silver medal, so small that I hadn't noticed it at first.

The envelope on top was unsealed. Inside was a wad of currency, both United States money and Mexican pesos. "Ohhhh!" Dee Dee said. "How much money is in there?"

I thumbed through it. "About a hundred and fifty dollars in U.S. bills. I don't know how much the pesos would be worth."

"Is there a name somewhere in there?"

I dropped the first envelope and medal into my lap and opened the second. Inside was a small pocket calendar, two years out-of-date. The names of the months and days of the week were in Spanish, each day crossed off with a tiny black *X* up through March second. From March third there were no markings on the calendar.

Dee Dee gasped. "March third is the day the murder took place! What do you think that means?"

83

"I don't know. Whoever owned these things must have left this house the day before."

"Or on the day of the murder."

"You mean that the person might have seen what happened?" I shivered, thinking of how terrifying that would be.

"What else have you got there?" Dee Dee asked.

With the calendar was a small envelope, addressed to Rosa Luiz at a post-office address someplace in Mexico called El Chapul, and there was a canceled Mexican stamp on the envelope.

Rosa? Is that your name? I felt a shiver of recognition. I turned the envelope over and stared at it. "This is a personal letter," I said. "I don't think we should read it."

"Sure we should!" Dee Dee demanded. She was practically leaning into my lap. "It's been opened, hasn't it? Besides, we need to know who owns these things, don't we?" She paused and added, "And if they have anything to do with the murder."

From the envelope I took out a small, rough sheet of paper. It was dated about four years ago and was addressed to Rosa Luiz with a formal heading.

"Can you read Spanish?" Dee Dee asked me.

"No."

"Then stop staring at the letter and give it to me. I'll read it."

Almost reluctantly I handed the sheet of paper to her, and she studied it. "Oh, dear," she said.

I reached over and shook her shoulder. "Read it aloud! I want to know what it says too!"

84

Dee Dee complied, translating as she went along, with only a few stumbles.

> This is to inform you that your uncle, Carlos Reyna, died last week of complications brought on by influenza. He worked on my farm for many years, as you may know. The other workers told me that you were his only living relation, so I am writing to inform you that he is buried in the church cemetery at Hermosillo. Señor Reyna had only a few possessions. I will hold them for you if you wish, but I am enclosing in this letter the medal he always wore.
>
> With sincere condolences,
> Señor Diego de la Ruiz,
> Rancho Playa del Rey, Sonora

Sorrow wrapped itself around me, its weight bending my shoulders. "Poor Rosa," I murmured. "She was all alone."

Dee Dee's glance was curious. "How do you know that?"

I was puzzled too. "I don't really know. I just—" I took a deep breath and tried to cover by saying, "I just took it for granted that if she were her uncle's only relative, then *he* must have been *her* only relative."

"Wrong," Dee Dee said. "She might have been married. She might have a dozen children, parents, brothers, sisters-in-law, who knows?" She paused. "The real question is who is this Rosa Luiz, and what are her things doing in this closet?"

"She probably worked here," I answered.

Dee Dee fingered the bills. "Poor thing. She worked hard for this money. She wouldn't have wanted to leave it behind. Maybe we could find her and get it back to her."

"We can't do that!"

"Why not? You sound so positive."

The presence who had contacted me was Rosa. I was sure of this. But I couldn't tell Dee Dee about it. How could I explain?

"I know what we can do," Dee Dee said. "We can telephone Mr. Holt. Maybe he'll know where Rosa is."

"No!" I insisted, but Dee Dee handed me the letter, jumped to her feet, and ran into the kitchen.

I hurried after her. "Dee Dee, wait a minute. I don't think telephoning Mr. Holt is a good idea."

But Dee Dee had already bent over the Houston telephone directory and was thumbing through the pages. "I know where Mr. Holt works," she said. "Yes, here's the number. I'll dial. You talk."

"We shouldn't . . ." I began, but Dee Dee had already finished dialing.

"Here," she said in a stage whisper, thrusting the receiver at me. "It's ringing!"

"Hello?" a masculine voice was saying as I reluctantly took the receiver from Dee Dee. "Hello?"

I tried to sound very businesslike, but I felt strange talking to a man whose son was a murderer. "My name is Sarah Darnell. Is this Mr. Martin Holt?"

"Yes, it is."

I plunged right in. "Mr. Holt, we're living in your former house on Fair Oaks Lane. We've found something that belongs to a Rosa Luiz, and I hope you can tell me how we can get in touch with her."

For a moment there was silence. "Mr. Holt?" I asked. "Are you still there?"

"Yes," he said, his voice so thick with suspicion that it dropped a notch. "What do you want? I don't understand the reason for this call."

"I'm sorry," I said. "Maybe I didn't explain it right. I was cleaning up, and I found a few possessions belonging to a Rosa Luiz."

"What possessions?"

I don't know why, but something kept me from telling him everything. "A small amount of money and a religious medal. Her name was with them."

"Oh," he said, the tension leaving his voice. "Well, somehow they must have gotten tucked out of sight and she forgot about them. Obviously they didn't mean much to her."

"You know her, then."

"Yes," he said.

"Did she work for you?"

"A long time ago. It must have been ten years, at least. I remember it was when we first moved into that house. We only employed her for a few months. She didn't work out."

I took a deep breath and tried to sound calm. "Do you know where she went?"

"No," he said. "Probably back to Mexico."

"I'd like to return these things to her."

"Forget it," he snapped. "She was one of the many illegals. She's probably somewhere back in Mexico, and

87

you'd never find her. Keep the money. Count it as an unexpected gift."

"That's all you can tell me about her?"

"That's more than enough. I scarcely remember her—" He broke off, his tone almost angry. "I have a business appointment. There's really nothing more we need to discuss, is there?"

"No," I said. "Thank you very much."

As I hung up the receiver Dee Dee leaned across the counter, asking eagerly, "Well? What did he say? Tell me!"

I tightly gripped the envelope that held Rosa Luiz's few possessions. "He said he barely remembered her, that she worked here for just a few months when they first moved into this house."

Dee Dee looked disappointed. "So that's that."

"Let's keep this to ourselves," I told her. "At least for now, I'd just as soon no one else knew about it."

Dee Dee tried to look innocent. "Sure, if you want. I can keep a secret, no matter what Eric says about me. But I don't understand why—"

"No real reason. Just humor me. Okay?"

But I did have a reason. The dates Mr. Holt gave me were years before the dates on the letter and on the calendar.

Martin Holt had lied to me, and I wanted to know why.

Chapter Seven

When Dee Dee left for lifeguard duty, I was glad. I needed time to think.

Mom handed me a folded newspaper. "Do me a favor and take this out to the garage," she said. As I glanced at the newspaper the front-page headlines gave me an idea.

"Do you think that the *Houston Post* or the *Houston Chronicle* would let me look up back copies of their newspapers?" I asked Mom.

"You can find back issues of local papers on film in any city's downtown library." She straightened, a hand at the small of her back, and leaned against the kitchen counter, studying me. "You want to read about the murder, don't you?"

"Yes."

Her forehead puckered. "I don't think that's a good idea."

"Everyone else knows all the details. I think it will be easier to know what happened here than to guess at it." I had to learn as much as possible about what really happened.

Mom hesitated. "Maybe we should ask your father for his opinion."

I walked over to face Mom, resting my hands on her shoulders. "Mom, you've got to stop worrying about me. I need to be independent. I have to make my own decisions."

Mom took a deep breath, closing her eyes. She opened them, looked right into my eyes, and said, "All right, Sarah. I trust your judgment. If you want to go to the library, you can take the car. I won't need it until late this afternoon."

"Thanks, Mom." I gave her a hug, then paused. "Do you happen to know how to get to the downtown library?"

She laughed. "Call them up, O Independent One. Ask *them* for directions."

■

"Let's try this one first," the librarian said as she snapped the first roll into place in one of the microfilm readers and showed me how to fast-forward and reverse. "As far as I remember, the issues that first tell about the murder are included in here. The stories about the trial are in the roll on the bottom of the stack I brought you." She studied me. "We haven't had anyone ask for these dates in a long time."

I just nodded. As she walked away I began to forward

the tape from page to page, rapidly scanning the front pages. The fast-forward made me sick to my stomach, and every now and then I had to pause, closing my eyes to give them a rest.

I found the story close to the middle of the film. It was under a top-of-the-page banner headline: DELIVERY GIRL BRUTALLY MURDERED; TEENAGER CAUGHT, CONFESSES.

The picture of Adam Holt was not very clear, and one arm was across his face, so a school photo from the year before was run next to it. Adam was blond and pudgy and looking away from the camera, unsmiling, so it was hard to tell about his eyes.

Basically there was not much more information in the news stories than Dad had told us. The murder victim, Darlene Garland, apparently came to the Holts' door with a pizza delivery. Adam Holt met her there with a knife. He attempted to drag her up the stairs, she bolted and tried to run, and he stabbed her.

The follow-up stories covered the same information. Adam told his story to two police officers while being driven to headquarters, but refused to give a written or taped confession after his parents hired an attorney.

I rewound the film, according to instructions, and put on the last roll—the one with the accounts of the trial. This one had some information that hadn't come out in the earlier stories. A woman who lived across the street from the Holts testified that she had been gardening in her backyard when she heard screams coming from what she thought was the Holt house. According to her testimony, she ran inside her own house and locked the door.

"Did you call the police?" the prosecuting attorney asked her.

"Oh, no," she answered. "At first I was afraid, but then I thought how I've never heard anything like that around here, and it had to have been—well, I thought it was kids just chasing around and acting silly. If that's all it was and I called the police, I'd look like a fool."

I stopped reading. If only she'd called the police, they could have placed Adam at the scene of the crime. I rubbed my eyes, which were beginning to ache, and went back to reading the newspaper stories.

The woman told the court that she thought she had remembered glancing at her kitchen clock, and she was pretty sure that it read one-fifteen. The defense attorney discredited her testimony, which must not have been hard to do, because the delivery girl couldn't have arrived on the scene much before one-thirty.

The medical examiner testified there were two kinds of blood found in the Holts' hallway, type A and type O. Darlene Garland had type O blood, and Adam had type A.

The discussion about the oral confession took up half a newspaper page. The judge allowed it, even though the defense attorney reminded him that under Texas law an oral confession was not admissible.

In a later issue I read that the jury had found Adam Holt guilty of murder in the first degree and that he was sentenced to life imprisonment. But his attorney filed an appeal, based on the wrongful admission of the oral confession.

I rewound the tape, knowing the rest of it. A higher court threw out the verdict, and Adam was released to live with one or both of his parents. There was plenty of evidence to place Adam at the scene of the murder, but an eyewitness was lacking, so he got away with his crime.

How did this all fit in with Rosa? I had the uncomfortable feeling that something I had read held a clue to the answer, but it eluded me, and I couldn't capture it.

A voice spoke next to me, startling me so that I jumped. "Did you find what you were looking for?"

I stared up at the librarian who had brought me the film. "I don't know," I answered. "I thought there would be something about . . ." A wisp of a thought tickled my mind, then disappeared before I could grasp it. What was it?

■

"Do me a favor. Peel some carrots," Mom called as she trotted past me on her way to the garage. "I forgot about lettuce and tomatoes for a salad, so I'm going to make a quick trip to the store."

I peeled the carrots, then wandered from the kitchen into the den, Dinky at my heels. The house was quiet, the sun slanting long, shimmering ribbons of light through the west windows. I walked to the edge of the entry hall, which was peaceful in the late-afternoon stillness and shadow. I found myself waiting, melting into the silence, as though it were expected of me. Why?

Slowly, like cold, creeping fingers against my skin,

came the awareness that some unseen being was with me. Terrified, I whispered, "Rosa? Is it you?"

Esto para usted.

From classroom Spanish I remembered the words *This is for you,* but I didn't know what Rosa meant. Slowly I sank to the tiles and sat cross-legged. "What is for me? Rosa, what do you want of me?" I asked. My whisper was so loud that I shrank from the sound, trembling.

Dinky crooned in the back of her throat, and her hair stood on end. With a shriek she bolted from the room.

In spite of my fear, I squeezed my eyes tightly shut, took a deep breath, and tried to concentrate. *Rosa,* I begged, *don't force me. I told you that I'd help you willingly.* There was no response, so I added, *I'm trying to reach you, but I don't know what step to take next. You'll have to tell me. You wanted me here. I'm here. I'm listening. I'm waiting.*

Silencio, por favor. Her words were soft and tearful, almost like an apology, and somehow I understood that Rosa had something she wanted to show me.

Slowly I began to feel the room changing around me. The air shifted, turned warmly damp and sour with fear, and Rosa's sobs became little drops of ice that slithered down my backbone. I was afraid to open my eyes, terrified of what I might see.

Suddenly, with the swiftness and shock of a slap, the sensation vanished. *Rosa?* I thought in surprise. *What happened? Are you here with me? Do you want to talk to me?*

I could feel her breath against my face, but it was agitated. Her plan had been interrupted.

I slumped with relief, as though I'd been held tightly by a string and suddenly let go. Even though she hadn't told me, I suspected that Rosa had been about to unleash the horror that clung to this room.

Rosa, I'm afraid. I'm scared to death, I told her. *I promised to help you, and I will. But please don't pull me into something I can't handle.*

I waited for an answer, but it didn't come. Instead I realized that I was being watched by someone close by, someone I knew was not Rosa.

I couldn't stand the tension. My eyelids flew open, and my head jerked toward the window next to the front door. I screamed as my eyes met those in the face that was staring in at me.

The figure waved and gestured. Through a haze I saw that it was only Dee Dee.

Stumbling, shaking, I managed to get to my feet and cross the hall to open the front door.

"I didn't mean to scare you," Dee Dee said. She shifted the large potted plant in her arms and put it on the hall table. "You look awful. You're so pale. I'm sorry." She clutched my shoulders and led me to the stairs, pushing me down. "Do you need to put your head between your knees?"

"I'm all right. I'm not going to faint." I took a couple of long, deep breaths and felt the color flood back into my cheeks.

"What in the world were you doing on the floor with

your eyes shut?" Dee Dee asked. "Yoga? Oh, I know. You were meditating."

Strange Sarah. Not again! Oh, please, not again! Embarrassed, I snapped, "It doesn't matter, does it? I didn't think I was on exhibit."

"Hey, look," Dee Dee explained. "Don't blame me for seeing you. Anybody who comes to the door can see inside your house. It would be hard not to."

She smiled. "And don't be embarrassed because I caught you meditating. Lots of people do it. I got into a weight-loss program last year that called for meditating, and I tried it, but I couldn't keep my mind on it, because I kept thinking about other things." She giggled. "If I were you, though, I'd do the meditating in your bedroom, where you'd have some privacy, and not in the entry hall." She sat on the stair beside me.

"Would you like to split a Coke?" I asked, desperate to change the subject.

"No thanks," Dee Dee said. "It's almost dinnertime. I just came over to deliver the plant from my mom to yours and to tell you something about those papers and things you found. I asked Lupita if she knew anybody over here named Rosa Luiz and she—"

"Dee Dee!" I interrupted. "I asked you not to tell anyone about those things."

She looked slightly guilty. "I didn't, really. I just asked her if she knew Rosa Luiz. I'm not going to talk about it to anyone else, honest."

"Okay. So what did Lupita tell you?"

"That's the strange part," Dee Dee said. "She acted real scared and kept rattling on in Spanish so fast, I

96

couldn't understand her. I did understand a couple of words, though—*immigration* and *deported.*"

"Rosa?"

"That must be what she meant."

"If Rosa had been deported, surely the officials would have let her take her belongings with her."

"She must have taken her clothes," Dee Dee said. "Maybe she forgot about the packet you found until after she was on a bus headed back to Mexico, and it was too late."

"Her money and the silver medal her uncle left her? Do you really think she'd forget those?"

"I don't know." Dee Dee leaned over and scratched at a tiny red spot on her ankle. "We're not going to find out anything from Lupita. That's what I wanted to tell you."

"You're wrong. We *did* find out something."

Dee Dee stopped scratching and straightened, looking at me with surprise. "What are you talking about?"

"It's simple," I said. "We found out that Lupita knew Rosa."

Chapter Eight

By the time dinner was over, I was exhausted. I watched TV in the den and woke up during the ten-o'clock news to find I'd been sleeping all evening.

"It's a good sign," I heard Dad saying. "Sarah's beginning to relax. We all need to. The murder is over and done with, and we can't let it affect our lives."

"It affects the way I feel about the people on this block," Mom said. "I can't help it." She glared at Evelyn Pritchard's potted plant, which I'd moved to the coffee table.

"I know." There was a pause and Dad said, "We could take Sarah's example too. She's already made friends in the neighborhood."

I stretched, yawned loudly, and sat up, pretending to have just awakened, so they wouldn't know that I'd overheard what they'd said. "It looks like I woke up just in time to go to bed," I told them.

Whispers from the Dead

"I'm afraid that after your long nap you won't be able to get to sleep," Mom said. "Would you like me to make you some hot cocoa? I'll be glad to stay up and chat with you."

"Thanks, but I don't need hot cocoa—or conversation, either. I feel as though I could sleep for a couple of weeks."

"Maybe you need vitamins," Mom began, but Dad and I shouted at her at the same time.

"Dorothy!"

"Mom!"

She laughed. "Okay. I'll back off."

I kissed Mom and Dad good night and climbed the stairs to my room. Once inside with the door shut, I opened the bottom drawer in my chest of drawers and took out the packet of things that belonged to Rosa. Separating them, I laid them out on top of the chest to examine them. The silver medal seemed to tug in my hand, so I opened my palm, exposing the medal to view.

Rosa? I asked, but there was no answer. The silver grew warm, probably from the heat of my body. I placed the medal beside the little calendar and reread the letter.

What had Rosa planned to show me this afternoon? I shuddered, pushing the question out of my mind. I didn't want to think about it. I was afraid that I knew.

I began to yawn again. My eyelids were heavy. I wrapped up the little bundle and tucked it back into the drawer. I showered, put on my pajamas, and literally fell into bed.

I dreamed about a young woman, not much older

than I. She sat near the foot of my bed, huddled inside a large, woven shawl. Her skin was a deep brown, her black hair pulled back tightly, and her dark eyes never left my face. The sorrow that drew her features into a tight mask was so intense that in sympathy I reached out to her.

She straightened and extended her hands to me. But as she sat upright the shawl fell back, and I saw that her body was soaked with blood. The dark blood dripped from her fingers onto mine, and I was helpless to pull away.

"No!" I tried to cry out.

"*¡Ayúdame!*" she pleaded.

Terrified, I tried to shout at her to go away, to run from those eyes that stared into mine. But I couldn't move or speak. Finally, desperately, a guttural, animal sound escaped through my lips, waking me. I was tangled in the sheet, my body drenched with sweat. Struggling, kicking away the sheet, I managed to sit up and turn on the bed lamp to chase away the last remnants of the nightmare.

There were no other sounds in the house, so it was obvious I didn't make enough noise to wake Mom and Dad. I slumped against the headboard, unable to get the picture of the woman out of my mind.

Rosa. It had to be.

I'd promised to help her and had opened my mind to her. I'd allowed her to come.

"Not in my dreams," I murmured aloud. "There has to be someplace where I can escape. Rosa, I don't want you to frighten me like this. Do you understand?"

100

There was a special silence, like a door closing softly, and I knew she had left.

I didn't understand the dream. Why had Rosa been covered with blood? What did she have to do with Darlene Garland's murder? What had really happened in this house? I squirmed back down under the sheet, punched at my pillow and rolled on my side. I ached for sleep but I was afraid to let go, afraid that Rosa might return.

■

The next day, after breakfast, Mom decided to hang pictures, and I helped her, the measuring and hammering and pounding mercifully driving all thoughts of the dream out of my head.

Around eleven she asked, "Where's Dee Dee? I thought she'd be over to see you."

"She said something about having to go shopping all day with her mother. This is Dee Dee's day off from her lifeguard job."

"Speaking of shopping," Mom said, "I've been making a list. Hardware, plumbing supplies, that sort of thing. It's going to take me all afternoon to find everything on my list. Want to come? Or would you rather stay home?"

I smiled at her. "Going to a plumbing-supply store is not my idea of real excitement. I could stay here and work and be of more help. Would you like me to unpack the books and put them in the bookcases? I know how you like them arranged."

"I'd love it if you'd take care of the books," Mom said. "I've been dreading that job."

The mail came, but no letter from Marcie. Why should I have expected one? I hadn't written to her, either. I'll write today, I promised myself. I'll tell her about Dee Dee. Maybe about Tony. But I knew I wouldn't. I was distancing myself, afraid to write a letter that might not be answered.

Mom left after lunch, and Dinky settled into a nap on the top box of those marked BOOKS. I moved Dinky to another perch. Upset at being moved, she narrowed her eyes and mewed a complaint, then pretended to go back to sleep.

I was so busy checking titles and reading snatches here and there that I jumped when the doorbell rang. Dinky rose majestically, flipping her tail with a snap of irritation.

Through the window by the door I saw Tony and stopped, catching my breath, as his eyes met mine. I smiled, not trying to hide my delight, and hurried to open the door.

"I was in the neighborhood and thought this would be a good time to meet your mother," Tony said as he stepped inside and shut the door.

The air turned cold, and the walls of the entry hall seemed to press inward. My head pounded and I silently screamed at Rosa, *No! Not now! Go away! You can't do this to me now!*

Gasping for breath, I grabbed Tony's hand and tugged him past the entry hall, through the dining room, and into the kitchen. I let go and leaned against the nearest counter, breathing heavily. Whatever I had felt in the entry hall had gone.

But Tony was studying me, and it surprised me that his eyes had narrowed in the same way that Dinky narrowed hers, with light seeming to gleam from under the lashes. "What's the matter, Sarah?" he asked me.

"Nothing. I'm fine." I tried to shrug off what had happened. "I've been working hard unpacking books. I guess I got a little out of breath." I opened the refrigerator door, wanting desperately to talk about something else. "How about a soft drink?"

"Sure," he said, "but I can only stay for a few minutes." He looked at his watch and glanced back through the living room. "Where's your mother?"

"Oh. Mom. She left to run errands. She won't be back for a few hours."

Tony smiled. Did I imagine that he looked relieved? "My bad timing," he said. "Well, as long as I'm here, I'll help you unpack the books."

"Thanks, but you said you could only stay a few minutes. You won't have time."

His smile was easy. "I'll make time."

We took our soft drinks into the den, and Tony worked beside me, making the job go much faster. Our conversation consisted of his asking, "Where do these go?" and my telling him, "On the bottom shelf over there" or "Right here, next to the gardening books," until he suddenly stopped, took the books I was holding out of my hands, and led me to the sofa.

"We need a break," he said. "I want a chance to talk

103

to you." He didn't let go of my hand, and I was glad. I didn't want him to.

"Tell me about yourself," Tony said.

"There's not much to tell. We used to live in Missouri until Dad was transferred here to Houston."

"That's not about *you*," he insisted, and leaned closer, staring into my eyes as though he could see what was in my mind. "I want to know about Sarah, the things that make her happy, the things she likes, even the things that frighten her." His voice was low, almost a whisper.

His question puzzled me. "Why should you want to know what frightens me?"

"Something frightens you," he said. He stroked my hand. "Look. You're trembling."

Maybe it was Tony who frightened me. Or the way he made me feel. I wasn't sure.

"If it's the house," he said, "maybe I can help you."

He leaned back, breaking the spell, and I took a long shuddering breath. "How could you help me?"

"You're forgetting. I know Adam. I know the story about the murder."

"Did Adam tell you why he did it?"

Tony threw me a quick sideways glance. "There wasn't much doubt. He was on medication for a couple of things—an antibiotic he was taking because of a viral infection and a steroid he was taking to build himself up for the football team. He'd been having trouble with depression, too, and a doctor had given him something for that. Adam said he was so over-medicated, he didn't know what he was doing."

104

"But murder?" I asked. "How could anyone not know he was killing someone?"

Tony bristled. "I'm on Adam's side," he said. "I don't want him to go to prison."

"There's not much chance of that, is there?" I knew I sounded bitter, because Tony gave me another sharp look.

He was quiet for a few minutes, then said, "I guess it's you I'm thinking of, Sarah, and not Adam. I don't like to think of your being frightened in this house. You're a very special person, and I want you to be happy, not afraid."

"I—I'll be all right."

Tony moved closer and put an arm around my shoulders.

"You were frightened of something when I got here. I could see it in your face. What was it?"

"It was just—well, a sensation I had. It went away."

Tony's hand on my arm was warm and firm. "If you want to talk about it, Sarah, I'll listen."

I would have loved to have been able to tell him everything that had happened to me, but of course I couldn't. Yet maybe there *was* something Tony could help me with. I asked him, "You came here to see Adam sometimes. Isn't that right?"

"Yes."

"Did you ever meet any of the Holts' household help?"

For just a second his fingers tightened on my arm, but he answered easily, "Sure. There were a couple of them over the years—maybe three."

105

"One named Rosa Luiz?"

"Rosa Luiz?" His voice was strained. "I don't know. I'm not sure. The name isn't familiar."

"She was young and slender with a small, narrow face and large eyes."

He sat upright, turned, and peered into my face. "How do you know what she looked like?"

Stunned, I fumbled for an answer. "I—I found some things that belonged to her. She'd hidden them away under a loose baseboard in the closet in the maid's room off the kitchen."

"What were these things?"

"Money—both pesos and United States currency; a letter telling her that her uncle had died, which was addressed to her at a Mexican address; a silver religious medal; and a calendar."

"A calendar! What kind of a calendar?"

"Just a small calendar, two years old. She'd marked off the days up to March third."

He paused for a minute, breathing heavily.

"What's the matter?" I asked him.

"Nothing's the matter," Tony said. "I'm just trying to remember, as you asked me to." Suddenly he added, "You didn't mention the photograph."

"There wasn't a photograph."

"Then how do you know what she looked like?"

I took a deep breath and the words tumbled out. "I saw the woman—Rosa—in a dream."

I hated myself for telling. I'd done it again. I waited for the wary, embarrassed look to come into Tony's eyes. But it didn't. Tony looked at me seriously. "A dream," he

106

murmured. "I seem to remember there *was* a young woman. I think her name could have been Rosa."

"When did she live here?"

He scowled, as though he were thinking hard. "How should I know?"

"I mean, was it a long time ago? A few years ago?" Why had I asked that? Was I testing him?

Tony leaned back against the sofa cushions, and his eyes narrowed again as he studied me. "The calendar you found should tell you that, shouldn't it?"

Embarrassed, I blushed. There was no way to explain.

"Time for me to be going," Tony said abruptly, and stood. He reached down for my hand and pulled me to my feet.

"Please don't be mad at me," I said. "I—I wasn't trying to trick you."

"Hey, it's okay," Tony said. "I told you I couldn't stay long. I'm going to be late as it is."

I looked at the clock in the VCR on top of the television set. "Mom should be home soon," I said. "I wish you could stay just a little while longer and meet her."

"Sorry." Tony stopped me as I turned to go toward the front door and placed his hands on my shoulders. "Sarah," he said, "I don't like to worry you, but I hope you've got Rosa's things well hidden."

"Hidden? Why?"

"Are they?"

"No. Not exactly. They're in the chest of drawers in my room, but no one goes in there but me." He looked so serious that it scared me. "Why are you telling me this?"

107

"Because no one should know about them. You haven't told anyone besides me, have you?"

"I telephoned Mr. Holt to ask him about Rosa and told him I'd found—well, some of her things. And Dee Dee knows. She was here when I found them. She translated the letter for me."

Tony sucked in his breath and muttered something. "I'm sorry Dee Dee knows. The fewer people the better."

"Why?"

"Why? Oh, because Dee Dee spills everything she knows."

"I asked her not to."

He shook his head. "There's no way of telling what those things of Rosa's mean. Probably nothing, but we ought to keep quiet about them."

"I don't understand."

"She would have headed back to Mexico," he said. "There'd be no way to find her, and in trying, you might stir up a lot of unnecessary trouble."

"For whom?"

"For Adam and his family," he said. "Probably for Rosa, too, since she was here illegally." He took a deep breath, and his eyes were so dark and demanding that I shivered. He added in a voice so soft, I had to strain to hear, "And maybe for you."

My voice cracked as I tried to talk. "Tony! Are you threatening me?"

"Oh, Sarah!" he said, as though I'd hurt him. "Don't think that. It wasn't a threat. What I said was only a warning."

Chapter Nine

Mom was disappointed that she had missed meeting Tony. "I wish he'd called in advance," she said.

"He didn't plan on coming. He just happened to be in the neighborhood," I told her.

A little wrinkle flickered between Mom's eyebrows. "Sarah, before you go out with Tony again, your father and I want to meet him."

"Sure," I answered quickly. "That's taken for granted."

"Just make sure Tony knows the rule."

"I will. You're going to like Tony, Mom. I promise." Smiling, I rummaged through the nearest brown paper bag and said, "Nothing interesting in here. When I was a little kid, you used to bring me a lollipop."

"Try the bag near the stove," she said with a grin. "No lollipops in it, but I think you'll settle for some red grapes. They look sweet enough to burst."

I washed the grapes, put them in a bowl, and Mom joined me, munching on a handful of grapes as she leaned against the counter. "I stopped off at the civic-club office," she said. "I signed up for a family membership at the swimming pool."

When I didn't answer, she added, "Whenever you're ready to go swimming again, Sarah, the pool will be there."

But I wasn't ready. Not yet.

■

Dee Dee came over the next morning. "I saw your names on the club roster!" she said to Mom and me. "Have you been swimming in the pool yet?"

"We haven't had a chance," Mom told her.

"There's no time like the present," Dee Dee said. "I'm subbing for another guard, so I've got to be at the pool in a few minutes. Why don't you come with me? It's a hot, beautiful day, and the water is going to feel wonderful."

"I'd love to," Mom said. She pushed a damp strand of hair back from her forehead and laughed. "It wasn't hard to talk me into it, was it?"

They turned toward me.

"I'll work on putting the books away. There aren't many left," I told them.

"No," Dee Dee said firmly. "Come with us. If you don't want to swim, no one's going to make you, but you can watch us having fun and work on your tan. If you don't have sunscreen, I'll lend you mine."

110

Mom didn't say a word. She just waited, but I could see the hope in her eyes.

"I'll come and watch," I answered, although I wished I could do anything else but. I'd bring a book. I'd read. I wouldn't have to look at the pool if I didn't want to.

"Try," Mom whispered when we arrived at the pool.

To please her I looked at the water and the people splashing and enjoying it, and did my best to tell myself I could enjoy it too. But I began to gasp with each breath, pressing my hands against the pain in my chest, remembering how my lungs had ached for air. I stumbled back to the safety and shade of a large oak tree, dropped to the grass with a shudder, and deliberately turned my back on the pool.

Mom swam laps for a while down at the deep end, then walked to where I was lying on my stomach and dripped onto my arms and book as she wrapped her hair in a towel.

As she sat beside me I scrambled to my feet and asked, "Ready to go home?"

"I'd like to sun for a while, then have another swim," she answered. "Would you mind?"

"Mom, I came. I tried. Now I want to go home."

"I'll go with you."

"You don't need to. In fact, I wish you wouldn't. Stay and enjoy your swim. I can walk home in a few minutes."

"It's awfully hot, Sarah. Take the car," she said.

"No, you drive it back. Really, I'd rather walk." I kissed her on top of her head, turned to wave to Dee Dee, and strode out of the pool area to the street. It took only a few minutes to walk home.

111

As I unlocked and opened the front door Dinky streaked past me, not even bothering to curl between my legs as she usually did.

"Dinky!" I called, but she sat in the middle of the front flower bed, her back to me as if I didn't exist. Only the rhythmic twitching of the tip of her tail showed me that she was upset. "Goofy cat," I told her. "What are you mad about now?"

I shut the front door against the heat and hurried to the kitchen for water. Houston in August was not the place to go walking.

A tiny sound alerted me, and I tried to place it. What was it? A footstep? A board moving overhead? Or was it the click of a door closing?

I waited, not breathing, listening intently, and began to sense that someone else was in the house.

My first thought was Rosa, but it wasn't Rosa's presence I felt. Whoever was in this house was a living person, not a spirit, and he was just as aware of me as I was of him.

I heard another light movement, almost too small to identify, but it was over my head. Someone was upstairs.

Frantically I tried to think of what to do. What if I bolted through the kitchen door to the backyard and circled the house and ran for help? But anger overrode my fear. Why should I let someone prowl through our house, helping himself to whatever he wanted? While I was going for help, he could get away! It wasn't fair!

As quietly as I could, I tiptoed to the kitchen telephone and dialed 911. In a low voice I gave the information to the police dispatcher. Okay. Now I could leave the house. I hung up and edged toward the back door, but the doorknob moved uselessly in my hand. The dead bolt was locked, and the key, which we left in the door, was gone!

I heard a sound that seemed to come from the head of the stairs. He was coming closer. I'd be trapped in the kitchen, and it would take too long to try to unlock a window and tug it open. If the intruder was on the stairs, he could intercept me before I reached the front door.

Maybe I could get to my parents' bathroom, lock myself inside, and climb out the window!

The phone rang. It would be the police dispatcher calling back, but there was no time to answer. I broke into a run, not even trying to be silent, and heard him do the same. As his footsteps clattered down the stairway and across the entry hall, I gave up hope of reaching that back bathroom. I dashed down the little hallway to the nearby guest bathroom, flung myself inside, slammed the door behind me, and locked it.

I leaned against the wall for support and waited in the darkness, not daring to turn on the light. It was easier to hear each separate sound in the dark. Unfortunately there was no window in this bathroom, no way I could escape.

I could see light under the door, where the sunlight reflected on the tiles. The pattern was broken as some-one stepped in front of the door and stood there. What was he going to do?

The light pattern shifted as he stepped away from the door.

I let out a long swoosh of air, suddenly aware that I

hadn't been breathing. I knew what I'd do in his place. I'd go to the kitchen and get a small screwdriver or a skewer—something long and thin—to put inside the hole in the center of the doorknob and jiggle the tumbler so the lock would open. I'd used that safety hole more than once when I was baby-sitting little children who could lock bathroom doors but couldn't open them.

If that was what he had in mind, then my only chance was to get out of here before he came back! My hand was so slippery with sweat that it slipped against the knob.

I hesitated, too fearful to move. What if he was just outside the door, waiting? I thought of Dinky, silently poised to pounce on the birds that flew to our front lawn.

Was the person on the other side of the door also waiting, crouched and ready to spring if I should open this door?

The sound of a footstep, and he was back. Under the door the light was once more broken by the shadow from his shoes. I pressed back against the wall, well aware that I had nothing with which to defend myself.

I thought I heard the doorknob move. But I heard something else—a police siren—and it was coming closer.

There was a hiss as whoever was outside the door took a sharp breath. He had to have heard the siren. His footsteps left the hallway, moving silently but quickly.

The siren was shrill as the police car swung into our driveway. Heedlessly I threw open the bathroom door and ran into the entry hall just as an officer knocked loudly on the front door.

Unable to stop shaking or to keep my teeth from

114

chattering, I led the two police officers into the house and tried to explain what had happened. It was hard to tell them apart. They were both of medium height with medium-brown hair and probably in their mid-thirties. They told me their names, but I was so scared, I couldn't remember them.

One searched upstairs, one down. They examined the front and back doors and some of the downstairs windows.

"There's no sign of an intruder in the house, and no sign of forced entry," one of them said. "Have you found anything missing?"

Embarrassed, because I hadn't thought to look, I took a quick tour of the house. Everything seemed to be in place. Mom's shoulder bag was lying on her bed; and the wallet, with money inside, was in place. I checked Mom's jewelry box. She didn't have much of the real stuff—just her watch and a couple of rings—but they hadn't been touched.

Upstairs was the same. Tiny dust motes drifted through the bands of sunlight that spilled from my window onto the carpet. Dinky, who had strolled in when I'd opened the door to the officers, paraded past me, jumped to the bed, and settled, her eyes accusing me of allowing her peace to be disturbed.

"What do you know about this, Dinky?" I asked her, but her only answer was to squeeze her eyes shut slowly and pretend I wasn't there.

"Did you actually see someone in the house?" the first officer asked me as I rejoined them downstairs.

"No. I just heard someone."

115

"Houses pop and creak with temperature changes. Maybe you heard the air conditioner start up."

"No. I heard footsteps. He—he was standing outside the bathroom door."

"Did he try to open the door?"

"I—I don't know."

"Did you see the doorknob move?"

"Not exactly. I—I didn't turn on the light."

They gave each other a patient look, and I felt my cheeks burn as my face reddened. "I didn't imagine it. Someone was here."

One of the officers gave me his business card and said, "If you have any more trouble, just call us."

"You don't believe me."

The other wiped the sweat from his forehead with the back of one hand and replaced his hat. "No sign of forced entry," he said, "and nothing missing, so far as you can tell. If it were someone burglarizing the house, he probably would have taken your mother's watch and rings. He'd definitely have taken the cash, and maybe the credit cards."

"I guess," I answered, but another thought hit me. "Unless he didn't come here to steal anything."

The officer with his hand on the doorknob paused and turned to look at me. "Have you had any strange phone calls? Anyone following you? Any reason to think you might be a target?"

"No."

The other officer nodded toward the card in my hand. It was obvious he was getting impatient. "Call us if you need us," he said.

116

"Thank you," I mumbled as they left the house. I knew they didn't believe me.

"Why was someone in this house?" I asked aloud. "Why? Why? Why?"

The next thought startled me: *Who?*

I didn't have the answer.

Chapter Ten

Mom and the police car passed each other as she drove into our street. I waited outside while she parked the car. I knew there'd be questions.

"It looked to me as though that police car came out of our driveway," Mom said before I had a chance to tell her a thing. Her suit was almost dry under the shirt she was wearing as a cover-up, and her towel was draped around her neck.

"It did," I said. "I called the police."

Mom stopped in mid-step and stared at me. "Why? What happened?"

"Come on inside. I'll tell you all about it."

She followed me into the house and back to the kitchen, asking, "Was someone trying to break in?" A sudden thought struck her, and she grabbed my shoulders, searching my face. "Sarah! You're all right, aren't you?"

"Mom!" I had to shout to get her to pay attention. "Stop asking so many questions! Just listen to me!"

"Tell me first about *you*," she demanded.

"I'm fine. No problems."

"Then what—?"

"Sit down, Mom, and give me a chance." I practically pushed her into the nearest kitchen chair and sat beside her. "When I came home, I went straight to the kitchen for a drink of water. While I was in the kitchen I thought I heard someone moving around upstairs, so I called the police."

"Did they catch him? Oh, my gosh!" Her right hand clasped her left wrist. "My watch! It was right there on the nightstand! And my handbag! The credit cards!" She was half out of her chair.

"Whoever it was didn't take anything," I assured her.

She looked puzzled and sat down again. "Nothing? Who was it? Did you see him?"

"No." I took a deep breath that ended in a sigh. "Mom, I know I heard someone run down the stairs. I locked myself in the guest bathroom, so I didn't see him, but I heard him."

"Why didn't you try to get away from him by running out the back door?" Mom asked. "That would have been quicker and safer."

"Because the dead bolt was locked and the key wasn't in the door."

We both looked at the door at the same time. "There it is," Mom said. "On the floor right under the lock."

"It wasn't there then! I would have seen it! That's why I ran to the bathroom. I heard him run down the stairs. He came down the hall toward the bathroom. I could even see his shadow when he stood in front of the door."

Mom's eyes were wide, and her mouth opened. "But—"

"Please don't interrupt. Let me tell you. I don't know if he was going to try to unlock the bathroom door or not. When he heard the police siren, he left."

"The police must have seen him."

"They didn't. They searched upstairs and downstairs and didn't find any sign of forced entry. And nothing was missing." Bitterly I added, "They practically said they thought I imagined the whole thing."

Mom looked troubled. She reached over and took my hand. "Is there any chance that you could have, Sarah? The key *is* there."

"No," I insisted.

Her glance was searching. "Sarah, you've never explained what frightened you when you first set foot in this house. Could what happened here today be tied in with that?" She took a deep breath, and I could see the fear in her eyes. "Does this all have anything to do with that spirit you once imagined was with you?"

"No!"

"Well, then," Mom said brightly, as though she were doing her best to support me, "I'll get out of this bathing suit and we'll take another look around." In spite of her words, I could see the doubt in her eyes, and it hurt.

In less than five minutes she returned, her hair still damp and uncombed. "I'll take the downstairs, you take

120

the upstairs," she said, and disappeared into the dining room, where I knew she'd count the silver.

I automatically went to my own room first. Nothing had been disturbed, including a handful of change I'd left on top of the chest. One by one I repeated the opening and checking of each drawer, starting at the top. Nothing had been touched. But as I tried to close the bottom drawer it seemed to stick, resisting my efforts. It was as though someone were tugging it out as I was trying to push it in. I suddenly stopped, and the drawer wobbled, jumping back an inch.

"Why are you doing—?" I didn't finish the question, because I suddenly knew the answer. I dropped to my knees and shoved both hands into the folded clothes, my fingers frantically groping for Rosa's packet.

It was no longer in the drawer. It was gone.

So angry that tears burned my eyes, I sat back on my heels. Whoever was in this house had stolen it!

Who would do such a thing?

My first thought was Tony, but I didn't know why it would have been Tony. No. It couldn't have been. He had even warned me to hide the packet.

Dee Dee knew about it. She'd seen Rosa's things, even read the letter, but there was no way she could have left her lifeguard job to break into our house.

But Dee Dee couldn't keep a secret. Tony had been concerned about this, and now I was too. I knew that she'd told Lupita about Rosa's things, and I bet she told Eric.

Could Eric have been the thief?

I closed the drawer, which offered no resistance now,

and walked into the short hallway that led to both bed-rooms. As I stood there, trying to sort out my thoughts, I stared ahead into the spare bedroom, watching a hot breeze ruffle the leaves of the tree outside the window. The curtain was caught in the sash.

My skin prickled as I realized what I was seeing. No one had opened this window—not with the air-conditioning on! Then how did the curtain get caught?

I rushed to the window and opened it, pulling the curtain aside. Below the window was a short ledge, and nearly touching the ledge was a long, thick branch of the tree that was centered in the narrow courtyard garden between this part of the front of the house and the garage.

I closed the window and tried to lock it, but the lock on top of the sash was loose and spun around. The metal piece into which it would have fastened was not on the sash. The minute Dad came home, I'd ask him to repair the lock. Until then— Frantically I looked around the room, trying to find something to wedge against the lower sash so the window wouldn't open, but I didn't see anything that would hold it.

My thoughts ran into and over each other so rapidly, it was hard to keep up. This had been Adam's room. His father must have known the lock was broken. Maybe Adam had broken it on purpose. For how many years had Adam sneaked in and out of this window? Mr. Holt lied to me about the years in which Rosa had worked for them. Had he told Adam what I'd found? Had Adam come back to steal the packet?

Adam, the murderer! Had he been the one I'd heard in the house?

But Eric had said that Adam went to California to live with his mother. If it wasn't Adam, it had to be Eric.

I ran toward the telephone in my room, sprawling across the bed. I flipped through the phone book with numb fingers until I found Eric's number, then dialed it.

"Hello," he said. I stared at the phone for a moment, unable to answer.

"Hello?" Eric said again. "Who's there?"

"I—it's me—Sarah."

"Sarah who?" he asked in a mocking tone.

I put all my fury and strength behind my words. "Eric, where is Adam Holt?"

He hesitated for only a moment. "I told you. He's living in California with his mother." He slipped into the mocking tone again. "Oh, I see. You want the name of the town. Forgot it, did you? Well, it's Cedar Creek." Patiently he spelled, "C-E-D-A-R—"

I interrupted. "It's a big joke to you, isn't it?"

"Big joke? I wouldn't know. I've never been there."

"Eric! You know what I mean. Why are you treating me like this?"

His voice softened just a little. "You haven't got much sense of humor, have you, Sarah?"

"Not when it comes to someone breaking into our house and scaring me to death."

"You don't sound dead. You sound extremely alive and healthy."

I took a deep breath and tried to keep from screaming at him. "Eric, are you lying to me?"

123

Joan Lowery Nixon

"Lying? About what?"

"Cut it out! Are you lying about Adam being in California?"

"Of course not," he said so smoothly, it was as though he were pretending to lie.

"I'm not going to get a straight answer out of you, am I?"

"Very few people do."

"You're covering up for Adam Holt, aren't you? Why are you on his side?"

He bit his words off angrily. "Why shouldn't I be? Adam wasn't convicted. That means he's free. So what's he supposed to do for the rest of his life—live somewhere he doesn't want to live, like an outcast?"

I tried to hold back a sob, but I couldn't. "Did you break into our house?" I asked him.

"Why should I do a thing like that?"

"The police were here. Didn't you see them?"

"No. I just got home. What happened?" He sounded more curious than concerned.

I rubbed furiously at my eyes with the back of one fist. "Someone was in the house when I came back from the pool."

"That's terrible. Did he steal anything?"

There was a false note in his voice, as though he were covering up. Covering what? I was determined to find out.

"Nothing was stolen," I said. "I was afraid he was after Rosa's things, but fortunately he didn't find them."

"But—!" His surprise slipped out before he could check it.

124

My trick had worked. Eric knew about Rosa's possessions, and he knew who'd come after them.

Was it Adam? Or Eric?

"You're no help. Thanks for nothing," I snapped at him, and hung up before he could say another word.

One more thing to look up in the telephone book— the area code for Cedar Creek, California. Directory assistance gave me a telephone number for Mrs. Martin Holt.

She answered on the third ring, and I was almost too nervous to talk. My voice came out in a squeak as I asked, "May I please speak to Adam?"

I heard her suck in her breath. There was a long pause and her voice was suspicious when she asked, "Who is this?"

"My name is Sarah."

"Do you have a last name, Sarah?"

"I'm sorry, ma'am. Sarah Darnell." I tried to mumble the last word, hoping she wouldn't hear it clearly and connect it with the buyers of her Houston house.

"Why do you want to talk to Adam?" she persisted. "Are you another reporter?"

"Oh, no!" Quickly I tried to reassure her. "I'm only sixteen. I'm in high school."

I had thought she'd be reassured, but the suspicion was still in her voice as she answered, "Where are you calling from?"

"I didn't mean to bother you," I said. "Please, could I talk to Adam?"

Her voice was sharp. "I'm sorry. Adam can't talk to you right now."

"Will he be back soon?"

"How should I know? I don't keep track of his hours," she snapped. "You can leave your number, but I can't guarantee if he'll return your call. Just don't keep calling and pestering me. Understand?"

"I understand," I said and hung up. I was sure now that Adam didn't live with his mother.

Slowly I walked down the stairs and sat on the bottom step, trying to sort out my thoughts. As I glanced at the window by the door I remembered how frightened I had been when I'd seen Dee Dee peering through it. "Anybody who comes to the door can see right inside the hall. It would be hard not to," Dee Dee had said.

So when Darlene Garland had come to the door with her pizza delivery, what had she seen?

Suppose that Adam Holt hadn't killed her because she resisted him, as he had claimed. Suppose he had killed her because she had witnessed something he hadn't wanted anyone to see.

Rosa's murder?

It seemed like a wild idea, but I became excited as it began to fit. I remembered that the woman who lived across the street from the Holts said she had heard screaming but had placed it earlier than the delivery girl's arrival. Had she heard Rosa screaming, and not Darlene?

Adam's parents hadn't called the police and had been in the house for at least twenty minutes before the police contacted them. Why? Had they suspected that Rosa had been murdered and tried to get rid of any trace of the woman? That would account for the time. If no

126

one knew of Rosa's presence, if she had come alone to the United States and had no family who knew her whereabouts, who would miss her? Who would know that she was gone?

I didn't have all the facts I needed, but I thought I knew where I could get them.

■

In the morning I borrowed the car from Mom, telling her only that I needed to go downtown again. It was my dumb good luck that when I reached the police administration building on Riesner and asked to speak to the detective in charge of the Adam Holt case, he was there and agreed to talk with me.

His name was Mark Hardison. He was stocky and slightly balding, and his face looked like weathered leather. "Sit down," Sergeant Hardison said, pointing to the chair across from his desk. "What can I do for you?"

I told him that we lived in Adam Holt's house. He raised one eyebrow, and I wondered if he felt the way we did about living in a house where a murder had taken place. "I need to ask you some questions," I said. "I've read all the newspaper accounts about Darlene Garland's murder and—"

"Why are you dwelling on the murder?" he asked. "Wouldn't it be a lot healthier to try to forget about it?"

"No," I insisted, "because I think—" I didn't want to tell him yet, and obviously I couldn't tell him everything. "Please let me ask you a couple of questions, and then I'll explain."

127

He nodded briefly, so I asked, "When Adam Holt was arrested, was he cut? Was he bleeding?"

"Aside from a couple of scratches made by fingernails, he wasn't hurt."

"But at the trial the medical examiner said they had found two blood types."

"That's right."

"How much blood of each type?"

He frowned. "We didn't ask that question. Offhand, it didn't seem relevant."

"You tested Adam's blood?"

"Of course. He's type A, the same as one of the samples found by the medical examiner."

"How do you know it was *his* blood, exactly? A lot of people are type A."

"It was tested for type only, as far as I know."

"Isn't there any way to test blood to make absolutely sure it came from a particular person?"

"There is now. There's a new way to match blood to a specific person through DNA, but we didn't have the information or equipment to take the tests at that time."

"Do you have the equipment now?"

"Not here in Houston. We can send samples to a lab in New York State."

"Could a test still be made from the sample you have?"

He leaned back in his chair and smiled. "The people who invented the process claim it could even be done on a mummy."

"On a mummy? I know I'm taking a lot of your time,"

128

I apologized, "but I'd really like to know what DNA is and how it works."

"No problem," he said. "It's not hard to explain. DNA —deoxyribonucleic acid—is in each cell of our bodies and is unlike that of everyone else's, so it's as accurate as a fingerprint. If a body's cells are badly decomposed, DNA can even be taken from bones or the pulp in teeth."

"That blood sample from the house may have been Adam's type, but I'm sure that it wasn't his blood."

"Just what are you getting at?"

"I think the blood came from a woman named Rosa Luiz."

He sat upright, and his eyes drilled into mine as he said, "That name never came up. Who is she?"

I told him about the packet belonging to Rosa and that it had been stolen from the house. I explained who I thought Rosa was.

"I know that everything wasn't in the newspaper stories, and that's why I came to you—to get some answers. There are too many things that don't add up. For instance, when I read the newspaper accounts of Darlene Garland's murder, it didn't make sense to me that Adam would have met her at the door with a knife and tried to force her inside. She was at the wrong address. He hadn't been expecting her. It wasn't as though he'd been lying in wait for her. But she would have seen him through the window when she rang the doorbell. She would have seen what was taking place in the entry hall."

"Seen what?" He leaned forward, listening intently.

129

"I think Darlene was an eyewitness to another murder. I think that she saw Adam kill Rosa Luiz." There! I'd said it! I let out a deep breath.

"I don't know where you got your information, but I think you're mistaken about this Rosa person. There was no sign that anyone besides the Holts was living in that house."

"What were the parents doing during the twenty minutes they were home before the police arrived? They had time to get rid of any evidence that Rosa had existed."

"We have no proof of that."

"We have proof that Rosa had lived there. The calendar—" I stopped. "Oh, no. I forgot it was stolen."

"We have only your word that those things exist."

"My friend next door saw them too. She translated the letter."

"Did you show these things to your parents?"

"No. I meant to. That is, I was going to show them after I added up all the facts and put them together."

"Do you watch a lot of television?" he asked. "Private-eye shows? Cops-and-robbers stuff?"

"I'm not making this up," I said. "Please take what I say seriously. There are other things that fit in. The woman who lived next door to the Holts heard the screams earlier than the time Darlene would have arrived at the Holts' house. Those must have been Rosa's screams."

"At the trial the defense attorney tore apart the neighbor's testimony without any trouble. She wasn't a credible witness. The time she estimated meant nothing." He shook his head. "The district attorney would like nothing better than to reopen the Holt case, believe me! But there'd be no way to make a strong enough case without someone who could place Adam Holt at the scene of the crime."

"Couldn't you question Martin Holt about Rosa? I know he lied to me about the dates she worked for them."

"What makes you think he wouldn't lie to me too?"

Discouraged and even a little angry, I slumped in my chair as Sergeant Hardison continued. "You have nothing to go on but guesswork concerning this Rosa Luiz. I have a clear recollection of the maid's room in that house. There was no bedding on the bed, and nothing in the dresser drawers. The room was clean, with no sign that anyone had occupied it for years. We had no reason to doubt the Holts on that one."

He stood, ending the conversation, so I had to stand too. "I'm sorry," he said. "They may have had an illegal alien working for them close to that time, but she could have left and gone back to Mexico months before the murder took place. You have some interesting ideas about what might have happened, but all you're doing is guessing. There's nothing tangible to go on."

I was halfway to the door of the homicide room when I remembered another question. "What about fingerprints?" I asked. "Darlene Garland was stabbed. Weren't Adam's fingerprints on the knife enough to help convict him?"

"They would have been a big help," he said. "Unfortunately the murder weapon was never found."

131

Chapter Eleven

When I got home, I found a note on the hall table from Mom. She'd walked to the pool and planned to be back by one-thirty or so. I'd just missed her. I could join her, but I didn't want to. Maybe I'd drive down to pick her up.

I didn't feel like eating lunch. I was tired and discouraged. I sat in Dad's reclining chair and tilted it back, closing my eyes. There was a plop as Dingy leapt into my lap. I stroked her head, scratching around her ears and chin, but her purr stopped suddenly, and I felt her hair rise and bristle.

"What is it, Dinky?" My hand dropped as Dinky shot from my lap with a guttural cry and streaked from the room. My mind seemed alert but my body wouldn't react. I tried to open my eyes but they were too heavy.

What was going on?

Gradually the room shifted, and the atmosphere

changed. The feel of the air, the way it smelled, even the furniture under me—it was all different.

Sarah. Venga acá, Sarah.

I remember the words, because a teacher had used them often: "Come here."

Venga acá. The voice that called to me from the entry hall was heavy with tears.

"Please, no!" I cried out. Terror spread from a cold lump inside my chest, shivering along my arms and down to my fingertips. My eyes opened to another room, another time. Reluctantly I rose from my chair and walked, one slow step after the other—as though I were an automaton—until I could see into the entry hall. I stopped, clinging to the door frame for support, trembling so hard that I was unable to go any farther. From where I was standing, I could see across the entry hall to the front door and the window next to it.

Once again the white marble tiles were yellowed with sunlight, and the room was decorated as it had been before, except that this time the crystal vase of sweet peas was upright.

Suddenly a scream tore the air, and I clapped my hands over my ears. Before me, I saw Rosa being dragged across the floor. Her blouse had been ripped off. Her skirt was torn. She was screaming, struggling against a tall blond boy who bent over her, his right hand clutching a kitchen knife. As he raised it high I ducked my head and screamed, too, screamed over and over and over, unable to stop.

Suddenly he yelled in surprise. I heard him run to the front door and throw it open. There were sounds of a scuffle, as though people were fighting, and through it all a woman's shouts for help.

I couldn't look, and I couldn't stop screaming.

The room swirled; I lost my balance and fell to the floor, crying and sobbing. I'd been shown the horror of what happened, and I hadn't wanted to see it!

Rosa's terrified voice shouted in my mind *¡Peligro! ¡Peligro!*

"Leave me alone!" I begged, gasping with shock as someone grabbed my shoulders and jerked me up from the floor. I opened my eyes to look into Tony's face.

"Stop screaming!" he shouted at me.

¡Peligro!

"The murders!" I cried, half out of my mind. "There was blood—blood everywhere! Rosa's blood and Darlene's blood!"

"Sarah! Stop it! What are you talking about?" Tony's face was pale and shocked.

I clutched his arms and hung on tightly. "Tony! I saw it! I saw him—Adam—attacking Rosa. It was just as I thought. Someone came. Darlene. Yes, it had to be Darlene. She could see through the window. Adam had to stop her from telling what she had seen!"

"You saw this?" he whispered. He dragged me to my feet. His hands were rough, and his eyes were wide with fear. "How could you see all this? Tell me! You weren't there when it happened!"

"Rosa," I tried to tell him, "she asked for my help. She wanted me to see—" I burst into tears and covered my face with my hands.

134

Tony stepped back from me. I could hear a frightened hiss of air between his teeth.

I felt arms wrapped around me, and I heard Mom ask, "What's going on here? What's the matter with Sarah?"

"It's not my fault!" Fear shook Tony's voice as he faced Mom. "I came and found her like this. She—she says she saw—saw something."

I held tight to Mom. "I saw the murders," I said, sobbing.

"Murders?" Mom sounded scared too. "Who are you?" she demanded of Tony. "What are you doing here?"

"I'm Tony—Anthony Harris," he said. "I came by to see Sarah, that's all. She was like this when I got here."

"Tony," Mom murmured as she recognized the name. "Of course. Sarah's told us about you."

"I—I'll clear out," Tony said. "I'll get out of your way."

"No," Mom told him. "Please sit down and wait for us, Tony. I want to talk to both you and Sarah."

Mom took charge, and I was glad to let her. She washed my face, brought me two aspirins and a glass of water, and settled me in the big reclining chair in the den.

Tony was sitting hunched forward, his hands clasped together, his forearms resting on his knees. "I'm sorry, Tony," I began, but he didn't look up or answer. He just shook his head. It wasn't supposed to be like this. I felt more miserable than ever.

As Mom sat down she turned to me and said, "I want

135

to know everything that happened here. You first, Sarah. Start at the very beginning."

What difference did it make now? There was no point in hiding it any longer. I started with the day we came to this house and told Mom and Tony everything I'd heard and seen, except for my conversation with the detective. I didn't know why. Maybe because he had discouraged me and I felt a little embarrassed about having gone to talk to him. By the time I'd finished describing the apparition, I was exhausted. I wished I could curl up and go to sleep, but Mom turned to Tony.

"I'd like to hear whatever you have to say about it, Tony."

He was so pale that the blue of his eyes stood out more sharply than ever, and the skin was stretched tightly over his knuckles as he gripped the arms of his chair. "I—I knew about the packet of Rosa's things," he said. "Sarah told me about it, and I warned her to hide it."

"Why?" Mom asked, interrupting.

"I'm not sure. I didn't know what it meant, but I was afraid it could be damaging to Adam."

"In what way?"

He shook his head. "I don't know. Adam's gone through enough, and I didn't want him disturbed by something that was useless and unimportant. I hoped that Sarah would keep the whole thing quiet."

"I don't think the calendar was unimportant," I insisted. "It showed that Rosa was here up to the time the murder took place."

136

"Are you sure what year was on that calendar?" Tony asked.

"Yes, I'm sure."

"Why didn't you show it to me?" Mom asked. "You didn't even tell me about it."

"I was going to, when I knew what it meant." My excuse seemed weak. I looked at Tony. "Tell me, if you know. Is Eric the one who stole the packet?"

"Why ask me?" Tony answered. "You'll have to ask Eric that one."

Mom's eyebrows dipped into a frown. "*Was* there a Rosa who worked here, Tony?"

"As I told Sarah, I think I remember a Rosa, but I don't remember when she worked here," he said.

Mom made a little puzzled sound. "Then Rosa isn't just a figment of Sarah's imagination, like—" She stopped.

"This is different, Mom!" I protested. "Besides the— the other presence—wasn't in my imagination, either."

Tony's gaze was filled with suspicion, and his voice was so low, I could barely hear it. "Do you talk to spirits? Are you some kind of a witch?"

"No!" I shouted. "Rosa called on me for help, and I promised to help her. I didn't know what it would mean. After I nearly died—" I turned to Mom, holding out my hands in despair. "Please, Mom. I can't talk about it. You tell him."

Mom explained to Tony about the aftermath of my near-death experience. When she finished, she came to me and gently rested a hand on my forehead, stroking back my hair. "There's no question about it. I'm going to

137

call Dr. Clark and ask him to recommend someone here in Houston who can help you. This hallucinating is very dangerous, Sarah, and we're going to get help immediately."

I knew I wasn't hallucinating, but I was too tired to argue about it, and the idea of turning my problems over to someone else was very appealing at the moment.

¡Ayúdame! Rosa's plea for help lingered. I could picture the slender young woman with the sorrowful eyes. With an ache I remembered my promise.

Mom held out a hand to Tony, who stood and shook hers solemnly. "I'm sorry we had to meet during such frightening circumstances," Mom told him. "Thank you for trying to help Sarah."

Obviously she was still trying to sort out the whole thing, so she turned before she reached the door to the kitchen. "When you arrived at our house, Sarah was in the grips of this hallucination," she said. "Is that right?"

"Yes," Tony answered.

"Then how did you get in?"

He paused for only a second. "I could see Sarah huddled on the floor. I tried the door, and fortunately it was unlocked, so I was able to get inside."

"The door was locked when I came home," Mom said. "I had to use my key to open it."

Tony's glance didn't waver. "Force of habit, I guess. I must have automatically turned the dead bolt as I shut the door."

"Of course." Mom nodded and managed to come up with a shaky smile. "I hope you understand that I'm just trying to get the whole picture. I *do* appreciate your help, Tony."

"I understand," he said, and Mom left the room.

While they were talking, I was trying hard to remember. I'd come home, unlocked the door, and entered the house. Hadn't I locked the door behind me? I was sure I had. Force of habit, as Tony said. Locking the door was just something I automatically did without thinking. Is that why I couldn't remember having done it?

But maybe I hadn't locked it. Tony must have been right about the door being unlocked. He'd gotten inside, hadn't he?

There was another possibility. In my mind I saw the window upstairs in the guest bedroom. Tony knew Adam. Did he know about the broken lock on Adam's bedroom window? Dad planned to buy the hardware for the lock today and fix it tonight. Tony could have entered through the window.

Tony walked over to stand before me, so I struggled to get to my feet. "Don't get up, Sarah," he protested, but I was already standing. "I'll go now. You don't need me here."

"I don't blame you for wanting to go," I mumbled. "I'm sorry about what happened. I'm sorry because—" I felt myself blushing, and I couldn't finish the sentence. After that awful scene he'd witnessed, I knew I'd never see Tony again. *Strange Sarah. Weird Sarah.* I wished I could hide.

But Tony surprised me by taking my chin and giving me a light kiss on the lips. His eyes were so blue, so wonderfully blue, that they hypnotized me. I didn't want to look away from them. "I'm only going so that you can rest," he said. "I'll be back."

"You asked if I was a witch," I whispered.

"Oh, Sarah!" He wrapped me tightly in his arms, and I could hear the beat of his heart. "I don't know what I said. We were all so scared. Forget it. Forget everything I said. Will you?"

"Yes." I was more than content to forget and stay close in his arms, but he stepped away.

"I'll call you soon," he said. "That's a promise."

Mom came back, walked Tony to the door, and I heard only the low murmur of their voices.

When she returned, she said, "I was able to talk to Dr. Clark immediately. He gave me the name of a Houston therapist and said the man has a very good reputation."

"Did you tell Dr. Clark about Rosa? About the murders?"

"No," she said. "I just told him you were having some frightening hallucinations."

"Mom, they're not—"

She interrupted nervously. "The doctor you'll be seeing is named Dr. Arnold Fulton. One of his patients had just canceled an appointment for ten tomorrow morning, and we got the time. Wasn't that fortunate?"

"Mom," I told her, "please don't be afraid."

"Afraid? Sweetheart, I'm terrified! I don't know why this is happening to you, and I want it to stop!"

"Maybe it would stop if I found out what Rosa wants."

Mom hugged me. "Sarah! Don't do this. You're hurt-

ing yourself, and that hurts your father and me. Whatever happened in this house is over and done with.
Please believe that."

I returned her hug, saying, "I don't want to hurt you,
Mom."

"I know you don't, Sarah. I put that badly," she said,
tears in her eyes too. She tried to smile. "Why don't you
go upstairs and take a nap?"

"I am awfully tired," I said. I could feel her eyes on
me as I walked slowly up the stairs.

The first thing I did was check the window in the
guest bedroom. It was closed, so it told me nothing. Had
it been opened? I took a wooden coat hanger out of the
closet and jammed it between the sash and the top of the
window. I wished I'd thought of that before. It wasn't a
tight fit, but I thought it would hold until Dad fixed
the lock.

As I walked into my own bedroom, a word kept
returning, flicking in and out of my mind like a persis-
tent little gnat: *¡Peligro!* I tried to wave it away, but I
couldn't ignore it. *¡Peligro!* the woman had called. What
did it mean?

I thumbed through the vocabulary list at the back of
my Spanish-English phrasebook and found the word
quickly. *¡Peligro!*—"Danger!"

I had seen a repeat—as though it were a film—of the
murders. Afterward I had lain on the floor, sobbing,
screaming, trying to escape the horror of what I had seen
and heard. A woman had cried out, *"¡Peligro!"* Danger!
But the murders had already happened, the scene was

141

over, and Tony was there to help me. It didn't fit. The warning was in the wrong place.

I didn't want to think about it any longer. My head hurt, and I was desperate for sleep. I flung back the blanket and sheet, kicked off my shoes, and climbed into bed, rolling myself into a tight ball. Mercifully, within seconds I felt myself dropping into sleep.

■

Dr. Arnold Fulton matched his office. He was middle-aged and slender, with a head of hair as full as his thick, brown beard. His furniture was expensive but nondescript, and it was all in browns and greens and beiges. It was designed to be restful. Dr. Fulton was beige and brown and restful too. He moved slowly, with precision, and his voice was soft. He asked Mom to wait in his "parlor" while he heard my story.

I began with the drowning and went right through to the horror of yesterday's apparition. He sat motionless, his greenish-gray eyes on mine, and—except for an occasional blink—he didn't move through the whole recital.

When I finished, I waited for him to speak. I waited so long that it made me uncomfortable. "Aren't you going to say something?" I finally asked.

"You've related a remarkable tale. I need time to assimilate it."

"Mom and Dad are worried about me. They want to help me, which is why I'm here. But I want to be honest with you. I promised Rosa I would help her, and I'm going to do it."

"How can you help Rosa?" he asked.

142

"I—I don't know yet," I said. "I think she'll let me know." I took a deep breath to hide my embarrassment. "Look, I know how all this sounds, but I believe in Rosa. I have to."

"Do you believe that your house is haunted?" The question startled me.

"Haunted? No, I hadn't thought— Why did you ask that?"

"You've related a story of a ghostly voice, noises, and apparitions."

I felt myself blush. "I didn't mean it to sound like that. I was talking about a person—Rosa."

"Who you believe is haunting you?"

"You make it seem like a horror movie."

He toyed with a pencil, spinning it up and down between his thumb and finger, and was silent for a few long minutes. Finally he said, "Houses are not haunted."

I interrupted angrily. "I just told you that I—"

In turn, he spoke before I could finish my sentence. "Houses are not haunted, Sarah. People are, and not by either preternatural or supernatural beings but by their own internal fears."

"Rosa Luiz is very real. I didn't know about her before we moved into that house. And don't forget the packet. It's real."

"Very well. We'll accept the fact that the packet exists. Can you see that the packet could, in itself, have been the stimulus for the scene that took place in your mind?"

"It could, I guess, but it wasn't."

"Sarah, would you describe yourself as a creative, imaginative person?"

"Yes, but—"

"Then the house and the occurrence could have been the vehicles that allowed you to manifest your own fears. Do you see what I'm getting at?"

"You mean, my fear of the water? My fear of dying?"

"It's possible."

"But why would I hear someone calling for help?"

"Think about it."

It doesn't take long to see what he's getting at. "Do you mean that *I'm* the one calling for help?"

Dr. Fulton didn't answer. He just waited, watching me.

"So I'm calling for help in solving my own problem. Okay. But what does that have to do with a murder?"

"Do you still dream about drowning?"

I was surprised. "Why, no. I guess not."

"When did the dreams of drowning stop?"

I had to think for a minute. "About the time we moved here."

"Do you think your fears have taken on a new form?"

"I—I don't think so. When I dreamed about Rosa, it was very different. Rosa was a real person. Don't you see?"

He stood and said, "Sarah, I'd like to help you work through this problem. I'll talk to your mother now and set up the next appointment. Is this agreeable to you?"

"Yes," I answered, simply because I didn't know what else to say.

Dr. Fulton talked to Mom, and she seemed less frantic and more relaxed as we left his office and began the drive home.

"He seemed like a nice, sympathetic person," Mom said.

"He thinks it's all in my imagination."

Mom took her eyes off the road for only a second to glance at me sharply. "He didn't say that."

"But he thinks it. I can tell," I said. "Mom, I didn't imagine Rosa and what I saw any more than I imagined the presence that used to follow me after I nearly drowned."

"Oh, sweetheart," Mom said quickly, "I like Dr. Fulton, and I know he'll be able to help you."

Mom seemed so hopeful, I didn't want to discourage her. "I guess that means I'd better try to conquer my fear of the water," I said. "Okay. I'll do my best."

"Good for you, Sarah." Mom beamed and reached over to pat my knee.

Sooner or later I was going to have to swim again, but I could still feel the dark water smothering me, holding me, while my heart pounded against my ears and my lungs exploded with pain.

I don't care what they believe, I thought. My fear of drowning didn't create Rosa. She's real, and she needs my help.

Chapter Twelve

Tony telephoned soon after we arrived home. "What did the therapist tell you?" he asked.

I attempted to make light of it. "He thinks it's just my imagination working overtime."

I expected Tony to laugh or kid about it, but he didn't. He was serious when he asked, "What did he say when you told him about Rosa?"

"He didn't seem to think Rosa was important. He was more interested in what he thinks is my overactive imagination."

"Will you see this doctor again?"

"Yes. Mom wants me to."

There was a pause, then Tony asked, "When you visit a therapist, you tell him everything, don't you?"

"Yes."

"So you'll talk about Rosa and what you saw? All the details?"

"I'll talk about it, and he'll help me get some meaning from it."

"What kind of meaning?"

"Well, for starters, he told me I could be haunted— great word, isn't it?" My laugh came out more of an embarrassed squeak. "Haunted by my own fears, that is," I went on, "which means my fear of drowning, my fear of even going near the water. So to make everyone happy I'll have to work on the problem. I guess I'll start with our neighborhood swimming pool."

"I have a better idea," Tony said. "I know a nice little lake, close to your part of Houston. There won't be a lot of people around to stare at you, as there would be at the pool, because the lake's on private property. I'll be in with you, and I'm a good swimmer. You won't need to go in any deeper than your ankles if you don't want to."

"What about the owners? We can't just sneak onto their property."

"Don't worry," he said. "The owners live in Dallas. This property is undeveloped land, still wooded and very pretty. A caretaker comes by now and then, but I've always managed to stay out of his way. There's a dirt road into the place, and the lake is close to the road. Will you come with me?"

I didn't want to answer. I had said I'd try, but it was a huge step to take. Sweat trickled down my backbone, and my mouth was too dry to speak.

Tony's voice was so low and soft, it made me shiver. "I want to help you, Sarah. Won't you let me?"

"Y-yes," I heard myself stammer. To be with Tony? My breath came a little faster. Oh, yes!

147

"Good. I'll be over in less than an hour."

"Today? Now? No, Tony. I have to think about it." I pressed a hand against my stomach, which was beginning to hurt.

"You've had months to think about it," he said. "You want to tackle your fear of the water. Well, then, do it. Your whole life will change when you prove to yourself that you're stronger than your fear."

I knew he was right. Procrastination wouldn't help. I clung to the telephone as though it were a lifeline, and managed to say, "All right. I'll be ready when you get here."

I put down the phone and found Mom in her bedroom, sorting through a box of old shoes and wrinkled clothes. "Why did I pack these?" she asked with a sigh. "They belong in a garage sale."

"Mom," I blurted out, "Tony asked me to go swimming with him. I said I would. He'll be here in about an hour."

Mom dropped the skirt she was refolding. Her mouth opened, and she was obviously so surprised that she couldn't speak.

"Everyone keeps telling me if I conquer my fears, I'll solve my problems. Tony said I should take the first step right now, without thinking about it, and I guess he's right."

Mom's eyes shone. "Good for you, Sarah!" she said. "Would you like me to go to the pool with you and Tony?"

"We're not going to the pool. It's a little lake Tony knows about. He says it's not far from here."

148

"A lake?"

"Mom, he said it's on private, undeveloped land, and there wouldn't be a lot of people around. I'd like that."

"Just you and Tony." Mom frowned. "Is he a good swimmer? Good enough?"

"You mean, if I get into trouble again?" I tried to reassure her. "Mom, I'm not planning to go out very far into the water. In fact, just getting my feet wet will probably be enough for the first time."

"I don't know," Mom said. "The pool might be a better choice."

I dropped on my back across her bed. "You don't know how hard it is to make myself do this. I was so scared at the whole idea of going swimming with Tony that I got sick to my stomach when he asked me. But I said I'd go, and now you don't want me to."

"Oh, Sarah, it's not that I don't want you to!" Mom hurried to say. "You can't believe how happy I am that you're going to try. I—I'm just not sure about Tony, that's all. I don't really know him. How good a swimmer is he? How reliable?"

I rolled on one side and propped my head on my elbow. "Forget it," I said. "We'll stay home. I hated the whole idea, anyway."

Mom sat beside me. "I handled this all wrong. I guess I worry too much about you, Sarah. I'm too protective. I have to allow you to make your own decisions. Sometimes I just don't know what to do."

I took her hand and held it tightly. "You're a good mother," I told her. "I know how hard all of this has been on you and Dad. I haven't wanted to give you extra

149

problems, and I'm sorry about what's been happening to me."

For a few moments we were both silent. Then Mom jumped to her feet, tugged me to mine, and said, "Tony will get here before you're ready. Better find your swimsuit."

I gave her a quick hug and ran up the stairs. As I passed the open door to the guest room I glanced at the window. The coat hanger was gone, and a shiny new window lock had been installed, thanks to Dad.

The phone rang, but I let Mom answer it. In a minute she called up to me, "Sarah, it's for you. It's Dee Dee."

"I don't have time to talk to her right now," I shouted. "Will you tell her that I'm going to the lake with Tony and that I'll call her later?"

I pulled my bathing suit from the back of the bottom drawer, stripped, pulled it on, and critically examined myself in the mirror. I was getting out of shape. A few weeks of swimming laps again . . . I had to smile. That thought must have been a good sign.

I reached for a shirt and shorts to wear over the suit and grabbed a couple of thick towels from the bathroom cabinet, surprised at my excitement. I detested the whole idea of going back into the water, but I was eager to see Tony again.

The phone rang as I was coming downstairs. Mom appeared and said, "For you. This time it's Eric."

Making a face, I told her, "I don't want to talk to Eric —now or ever. You can tell him that if you want to."

"I'm not going to tell him that," Mom said. "I'll just tell him you're unable to come to the phone right now."

When she returned, I asked, "Did Eric say what he wanted?"

"No," Mom answered, "but he made me promise that I'd tell you to call him as soon as possible. He sounded so urgent, he must have something important in mind."

"That's *his* problem," I said, and glanced into the hall mirror, giving myself a smile of approval. My red shirt looked good with my dark hair. I wanted to look especially nice for Tony.

■

As we drove toward the lake Tony said, "I hope I satisfied your mother that I'm a good swimmer. I think she wanted to come with us."

"I'm glad she didn't," I murmured, almost too shy to say it.

"I didn't want her to come, either," he said in his low, soft voice, which never failed to make me shiver. "I wanted the chance to be alone with you, Sarah."

I loved the way he said my name. My heart gave a little jump. "Tony, don't be mad at me if I don't swim with you," I told him. "I'm really terrified of going into the water, so I may chicken out and disappoint you— and Mom."

He smiled. "You won't disappoint me. I can't speak for your mother, though. I don't know how she thinks, but I'm pretty sure we don't see eye to eye on everything."

I was surprised. "What do you mean?"

"I can tell she's counting on what your therapist said,

about you being haunted by your own fears. But I don't think I agree with her on that."

"You don't? Why not?"

"Because you described things with such detail— even what Rosa looked like."

"Then you remember Rosa?" I sat up a little straighter.

"Yes, I do . . . now. I believe you, Sarah. I believe everything you said."

"Thanks." It was the only word that came out. It would have been impossible to tell Tony how happy he'd made me. If I were Dinky, I'd have curled up and purred.

We turned off the paved street onto a dirt road. Tony decreased his speed, because the rode was bumpy as it led into a canopy of trees and thick underbrush. "There are berries in there," Tony said, "but it's too hard to pick them, and you have to watch out for snakes."

"Snakes? There aren't going to be snakes where we're going, are there?"

"No snakes. There's a nice clearing there. I promise you. You'll like it."

The trees created an arch of deep shade, cutting off the intense heat of the August sun. The woods we were driving through were quiet and pretty, and Tony was right. I liked this place very much.

"Tell me more about what you've seen and heard," he said.

"I told you and Mom everything."

"But didn't this Rosa talk to you about what happened to her? Didn't she tell you things?"

"She showed me, instead of telling me, maybe because of our language barrier. She's only spoken a few words, and some of those I've had to look up and translate because they were in Spanish."

"Words like what?"

"Oh—*ayúdame.* That means 'help.' That was the first thing she said to me. Then she asked me, 'Try to find it,' and yesterday she cried out, 'Danger!' "

"Yesterday? While she was showing you how her murder took place?"

"No. Afterward. It was all mixed up—the tears and the screaming and the blood, and you were there, helping me."

The car wobbled as we dipped into a rut, and Tony fought the wheel until we landed on firmer ground. "Has Rosa appeared to you since then?" he asked.

"No."

"But she could if you wanted her to, because you're a psychic, aren't you, Sarah?"

"No!" I stared at Tony, but he didn't look at me. He kept his eyes on the narrow, curving road. "I'm not a psychic," I insisted. "I have no control over any of this. I can only guess that somehow I still must have a link to the next world, and Rosa knows this and is using it."

"Why?" he asks.

"I'm not sure."

"I think I know. It's so you can prove that Adam murdered her."

"How can I? You—and maybe Dee Dee—are the only ones who believe that Rosa even existed. No one else believes me, so how could I possibly prove something like that?"

He stopped the car and turned to face me. "Knowing you, Sarah, I'm sure you'll find a way."

"Tony, I realize that you and Adam are friends, but—"

Tony didn't answer. He climbed out of the car, crossed to my side, and opened the door. "Come on," he said, and held out a hand.

"Where's the lake?" I asked.

"Just beyond that grove of trees. See the path? We'll follow it."

He held my hand firmly and walked ahead. I stumbled along behind him. The underbrush smelled moist and sour with decaying leaves. A low branch brushed my cheek, and I ducked, calling out to Tony, "Not so fast!"

"I'm sorry," he said, and put an arm around my shoulders, steadying me. "The path widens here. We're almost in the clearing."

In less than a minute we stepped into an open, shaded, sandy place with a small, crescent-shaped beach. The gray-green, glimmering water of the lake slapped against the sand with a comforting pat, and a few ducks sailed like toy boats across the water in the sunlight. It should have been a peaceful spot, but it wasn't.

Tony moved aside, and I was aware that he was watching me carefully. I wanted to ask him why, but I suddenly began to tremble as a terrible chill shook my body. My chest hurt as though someone were squeezing it; and my heartbeat pounded so hard, for a moment I grew dizzy. I was caught in a giant web of horror, each

154

sticky strand clinging, binding me so that I could never get away.

In terror I pressed my hands over my eyes and cried out, "Tony! What is this place? What's wrong here?"

He scooped me up in his arms and carried me across the clearing to the beach. Gradually the bright sunlight burned away the fear.

"I—I can stand up now," I said, stammering.

He put me on my feet, stood back, and studied me. "You had another psychic experience, didn't you?" he asked. "What was it? What did you see?"

"Nothing," I answered. "But I felt something. It was horrible, terrifying."

"What was it?" He gripped my arms so tightly that I struggled to free myself.

"Let go! You're hurting me!" Tony dropped his hands, and I rubbed my arms. "I told you, I didn't see or hear anything. It was just a feeling." A tear slid down my cheek, and I wiped it away with the back of one hand. My face was damp, and I hadn't even known I'd been crying.

"I'm sorry, Sarah," Tony said. He sighed. "About everything."

"Why did you bring me here?"

His expression was one of surprise and hurt. "Because I love this place. It's special to me. I wanted to share it with you because you're special to me too."

I didn't expect this answer. It confused me. "Please, let's go home," I begged.

"Go home?" Tony smiled reassuringly. "What happened to you shook us both up. Okay? But the feeling

155

you had is over now, isn't it? We don't want it to ruin the rest of our day."

"I don't think I can go swimming now. I've lost all my courage."

"You don't have to swim. Just take off your shoes and the clothes you're wearing over your bathing suit and sit at the edge of the water. You can watch me swim, and if you feel like it, you can at least wade in and get your toes wet." He pulled off his shirt and the jeans he was wearing over his swim trunks. As I hesitated, he said, "Won't you do it just to please me, Sarah?"

His eyes were so blue, so intense. "Just to please you," I echoed, and kicked off my sandals. I dropped the towels and tossed my shirt and shorts on top of them.

"You're a beautiful girl, Sarah," Tony said, "and a good person. You've never known what it's like to battle with evil. I don't think you could even recognize it."

"I—I don't know what you mean."

"It's just as well that you never find out."

"Tony? You're scaring me. Are you talking about Adam?"

"Don't try to judge Adam. You'd never be able to understand him."

I didn't like this conversation. Nervously I said, "Go ahead, Tony. Go swimming, and I'll watch."

But he moved a step closer to me until our bodies were touching, held me in his arms, and kissed me. I'd never been kissed like that. I'd never responded the way I was responding to him, with an eagerness that over-whelmed me.

The kiss went on—I didn't want it ever to stop—

156

while Tony lifted me into his arms and began to carry me.

It was hard to break the spell, but something warned me, and I pulled away from the kiss. Tony was walking into the lake.

"Take me back!" I cried out.

"No, Sarah," Tony said.

"You promised I wouldn't have to go into the water! Tony! Put me down! Take me back!" I began to kick and twist and push against his chest, but Tony was much stronger than I was. He gripped my free arm around the wrist and continued to walk.

It was hard to breathe, hard to see through the blackness of terror. "Help!" I shrieked in panic, even though I knew there was no one around to hear.

Chapter
Thirteen

Behind us came the sound of heavy, running feet, and a voice yelled, "Hey! You kids! Get out of there!"

Tony whirled in astonishment, and I twisted in his arms toward the voice. Standing on the bank was a heavyset man dressed in jeans and a faded, sweat-stained, cotton work shirt. "You're trespassin'! This is private property! Go do your swimmin' somewhere else!" he shouted at us.

Tony gave me a quick glance. I deliberately remained silent, and I could feel some of the tension leave his muscles. "Okay," he called to the man. "No harm meant. We'll get out." He carried me to the bank and put me on my feet.

Red with embarrassment under the man's gaze, I pulled my shorts and shirt on over my swimsuit and tugged on my sandals.

"Good thing I was warned to watch for trespassers. I

caught you just in time," the man muttered, some of his anger spent. "That lake's no place for swimmin'. Looks good on the surface, but it's a tangle of roots and vines underneath. 'Sides, I killed more than a few cotton-mouths in there over the past few summers."

Tony fastened the last button on his shirt and smiled at the guard. "I've been swimming here before," he said. "I had no idea the lake was dangerous."

"Well, now you know. Don't come around here no more," the guard warned. "You got that?"

We marched ahead of him, Tony pulling me across the clearing at a fast clip. The horror of the place reached up to entrap me, but it had no chance because Tony jerked me away from it. The guard didn't react to whatever terrible thing was there. Tony didn't. Why did I?

As we reached the car I mumbled at Tony, "I'll walk home."

"You can't do that," he said curtly, and opened the door, waiting for me. "Get in."

"Hurry up," the guard said to me. "I ain't got all day."

"I hate you!" I snapped at Tony as I climbed into the car and huddled against the seat. I *did* hate him for lying to me, for tricking me. And yet, as he walked in front of the car and I looked at him, I knew that if he were to kiss me again, I'd respond just as ardently. Why did he have such a hold over me?

Tony didn't say a word until we left the woods and were on the road. Then he simply said, "I'm glad the guard came when he did."

"*You're* glad! Not as glad as I am! You lied to me, and I trusted you! What a dumb trick, to try to force me into the water! That wouldn't have helped! It would have made everything worse!"

He glanced at me sharply, questioningly, but I wasn't through. "It would have been the same, horrible death! I was caught and trapped in vines before! I can still feel them wrapped around my arms and ankles! And my lungs! I can feel—" I pressed my hands against my chest, trying to push away the pain. "You could have killed us both!" I was crying again, uncontrollably, and I didn't care.

My storm of tears passed before we arrived at our house. Tony pulled into the driveway, turned off the ignition, and stared down at his hands, which rested on the steering wheel.

"I made a mistake," he said quietly.

"Lying to me was the worst part of it. I could never trust you again!"

"I don't blame you."

He looked so dejected that I wanted to relent. His gaze rose until he looked into my eyes, and I felt myself drawn forward, dazzled by the depth of that alluring, vibrant blue. Before I could give in, I threw open the car door, jumped out, and hurried toward the house.

He didn't call out to me. He didn't say he'd see me again. I wanted him to say it. No. I didn't. I heard Tony's car drive away as I fumbled with my key in the lock, and I didn't turn to look.

Mom heard me and came from the kitchen, talking all the way. "Sarah, Eric called again and was very upset

160

to find out you'd gone without returning his call. He didn't say what he wanted, but maybe you'd better call—" She was close enough to see my face and broke off in mid-sentence. "You've been crying! What's the matter?"

"We had an argument," I answered. I didn't want to tell Mom all of it. It would only upset her, and I'd hate to talk about it.

She nodded, understanding my mood, but I saw her take in the dry towels. "You didn't go into the water?"

"Not this time," I said. "I think you're right. I should start with the swimming pool." Heading off any further conversation, I quickly added, "I'm going upstairs to take a shower."

The warm water soothed away the remnants of my anger. I dressed in clean clothes and flopped facedown across my bed. Maybe I'd take a nap before dinner. There should be enough time. The room was cool and comfortable, the quilt under me was soft, and I drowsed toward the edge of sleep.

La fotografía. The word swirled into my head, demanding my attention, chasing away all chance of rest.

Groaning, I rolled over onto my back and sat up. *Rosa, there was no photograph. No* fotografía. *The calendar, the letter from your uncle, the money. Oh—and the medal. That was all.*

The air was agitated against my cheek. *¡La fotografía!*

It dawned on me that Rosa might be referring to someone else's photograph. "Whose photograph?" I asked aloud, the thought surprising me. "Adam's?"

The air was still. I'd given her the answer she wanted.

I had seen the newspaper photo of Adam taken in the corridor of the police station, as well as his school photograph. Neither was a very good shot. Where would I be able to find others?

From Eric? Would he have some snapshots? Forget Eric. I wasn't going to ask him for anything.

Suddenly I realized who would have photographs of Adam Holt. Sergeant Mark Hardison. Surely he'd have the official police photographs in his file. If I asked, maybe he'd let me see them.

But he'd want a reason, and what reason could I possibly give him? I didn't know why Rosa wanted me to look at Adam's photographs. I tried to picture Rosa in my mind. I tried to make mental contact. *Can you tell me why?* I asked her.

There was no answer.

■

Dee Dee called after dinner. "Okay, tell me all about it! What lake was it? How far out did you go? Were you scared? Could you handle it? I wanted to start you out in the swimming pool, and as I said, I'd be with you, and I'm a good swimmer, but if you—"

"Dee Dee," I interrupted, "I didn't make it. I'm back to zero."

There was a pause before Dee Dee, in her most cheerful voice, said, "Oh, don't look at it that way. It just proves I was right. A swimming pool is a lot easier to get into than a lake. When you're ready, we'll try again."

"Thanks. You're a real friend." I needed a friend.

162

"Do you want to do something tomorrow morning? I haven't talked to you for two whole days, and to begin with, I want to hear more about this Tony. Do you really like him? You never did tell me—is he handsome?"

"We had an argument. I may never see him again."

"Oops! Sorry. I *would* say the wrong thing. Well, how about tomorrow? Why don't we go over to Town and Country Mall? Anytime. I'm off duty tomorrow."

"That sounds good," I answered, "but there's someone I have to see first."

"Oh, who?"

Just like Dee Dee to be so blunt. I started to hedge a bit until I remembered that, on the other hand, Dee Dee might be able to help.

"Someone who might have some photographs of Adam Holt. Do you have any?"

"Good heavens, no! And I wouldn't want any, either!" Her voice dropped. "Sarah, why don't you forget about that murder? Thinking about it doesn't do any good."

"I will," I told her. "I promise. It's just that I need to see his photograph."

"You didn't tell me why."

"I'm not sure myself. Just trust me, okay? And, Dee Dee—don't tell anyone about it."

"Never!" she said. "I can keep a secret—well, as long as I'm told it's a secret. I mean, I told Eric about your going swimming with Tony at a lake because your mother didn't tell me it was a secret, and I didn't see why it would be. Say—where is that lake, anyway?"

163

"Not far from here," I told her. "I don't even want to think about it, so let's not talk about it."

"Where are you going to go to find pictures of Adam?" she asked. "I'll go with you."

A tickle of warning touched the back of my neck. "I'll figure that out tomorrow," I said, "and you can come with me if you like. I'll call you back and tell you what time." I didn't mean to be using Dee Dee for my own purposes, but I wanted to introduce Dee Dee to Sergeant Hardison. She could tell him that she had seen the packet of Rosa's things so he wouldn't think I'd invented it.

■

Sergeant Hardison agreed to talk to me. He couldn't see me at nine A.M. I called Dee Dee right away and said, "I made the appointment for tomorrow morning."

"What time?"

Again I felt a flicker of caution. "Expect me about nine."

The next morning I arrived at Dee Dee's house at eight, Mom's car keys in hand.

"Of course I don't mind if you take the car," Mom had told me. "You and Dee Dee have fun. Just don't plan anything with her for tomorrow morning, though. You've got another appointment with Dr. Fulton."

I found Dee Dee still in her dinosaur T-shirt, doing exercises.

"Nothing I do takes off a single pound," she complained.

164

"Get dressed," I said. "We have to be downtown at nine."

"I thought you said you'd be here at nine. Where are we going?"

"I'll tell you on the way."

"Why are you being so mysterious?" she asked.

Mrs. Pritchard came into the room. She gave me a wary look. "Good morning, Sarah," she said.

"Good morning," I answered.

Something was bothering her. I didn't need to wonder what it was, because she came right out with it. "What's all this about your needing some photographs of Adam Holt?"

"I want to know what he looks like," I answered.

"There were pictures of Adam in the newspaper and on television," she said. "Weren't they enough?"

"The newspaper shots weren't very good, and I wasn't here to see the news on television."

She was still suspicious. "This isn't something concerning your father or mother, is it? I hope they understand that everything about the sale was legal and correct."

"This is my idea only," I said firmly. "My parents believe in being honest and straightforward about everything they do."

She had the grace to look slightly embarrassed, as did Dee Dee.

But Mrs. Pritchard collected herself quickly. "See you girls later," she said with a quick wave of her hand, and breezed out of the room.

I looked right into Dee Dee's eyes. "That's why," I said.

"Well, it's different with parents," Dee Dee explained. "You're supposed to tell them things."

"Hurry up and get dressed," I reminded her. "We have to leave in about ten minutes."

■

I introduced Dee Dee to Sergeant Hardison, and he led us into one of the interrogation rooms, seating himself across the desk from us.

"That packet belonging to Rosa Luiz I told you about," I said right away, "Dee Dee saw it too."

"Yes," Dee Dee told him. "I translated the letter from Rosa's uncle."

"I wanted to prove to you it wasn't in my imagination."

"I had no reason to disbelieve you," he said.

"Is this where you take criminals?" Dee Dee asked. She looked around the tiny cubicle in wonder.

"That's right. But it's a good place to talk to attorneys, parents of juveniles who've been arrested, and—right now—you two." He turned to me. "I pulled Adam Holt's ID from the file. Suppose you tell me why you want to see it."

I couldn't tell Sergeant Hardison everything, and I didn't know quite how to begin. Trying to feel him out, I answered, "I read once about psychics working with the police in solving crimes. Do you believe in help from—well, from the other side?"

One eyebrow rose. "Can't say I do or I don't. I've

166

seen some unusual results—very unusual—but there's nothing scientific about it. We do check out almost all leads when we're working on a case, and this includes information from psychics."

Dee Dee stared at me, her mouth open.

"I'm asking you to trust me," I told Sergeant Hardison. "I'm definitely *not* a psychic, but I've had a strong feeling that I should see some clearer photos of Adam Holt than those in the newspaper. If I see the pictures, maybe I'll understand the reason."

He reached into a drawer and pulled out a photocopy of an official ID sheet. At the top were two, clear, close-up black-and-white photos of Adam Holt, one full-faced and one in profile. Under the photos was a form in which a complete description was written.

Dee Dee leaned over my shoulder to read the sheet, while I studied the photographs. I saw a pale, pasty-faced, pudgy boy with hair as light as his skin. In the shot in which he faced the camera his eyes were large. There was something about the eyes in that unfamiliar face—

I looked down on the list. Height . . . weight . . . color of eyes . . . blue!

"Do you have a pencil?" I asked Sergeant Hardison. "I'd like to darken the hair on this picture."

He reached into the drawer of his desk and pulled out a carton of colored pencils. "How about these?"

"Great," I said. I took a dark brown pencil and lightly shaded in the cheeks and chin, making the face look thinner. Then I pressed down to color the hair a dark brown and added a mustache.

"He looks like . . . like . . ." I made the eyes in the

photo blue, and I was positive. As all my questions about Adam suddenly came up with answers, shock blurred my vision, and I could hardly see. "Could I please have a drink of water?" I whispered.

"Right away." As the detective left to get the water Dee Dee pulled the sheet of paper from under my hand and continued to read it. "This description covers everything—even the purple birthmark on Adam's wrist."

"Tony," I murmured.

"No, Adam." Her voice was puzzled.

"Tony *is* Adam."

Sergeant Hardison came back with the water, and I gulped it gratefully. "Are you all right?" he asked, sounding concerned.

"Yes, thanks," I said, but my attention was on Dee Dee. "Did you tell Eric that we were going to see some pictures of Adam?"

"Me?" she squeaked. As I stared at her she slumped. "I didn't plan on telling him," she said. "It just kind of came out. I mean, it wasn't much of a secret. I didn't tell him where we were going, or anything like that, because I didn't know."

I jumped from my chair. "Sergeant Hardison," I said, "Adam Holt is in disguise as Anthony Harris. He looks like this." I shoved the ID sheet at him. "I realize now that yesterday Tony—Adam—tried to kill me. He would have succeeded, but someone—I'm pretty sure it was Eric—interfered."

Tears came to my eyes, and I had to gulp hard before I could continue. "We have to find out from Eric where Tony is now. If Eric's told him I'm looking for Adam's photographs, then he'll probably try to leave Houston and hide."

"Just because you could break his new identity?" Sergeant Hardison asked. "That's not sufficient reason."

"No. Because I know about the second murder, and I know"—I could see the clearing next to the lake in my mind, remembering the horror, and I shuddered, aware for the first time of what it meant—"I know where he buried Rosa's body."

Sergeant Hardison gave me an odd look. "You said a few minutes ago that Adam Holt tried to kill you."

"Yes."

He frowned. "We have to accept the possibility that he might try again."

It hit me like a sock in the stomach. "If he came to my house, I wouldn't be there, but Mom would! I don't want him to hurt my mother!"

"I'll call her," he said.

"Tell her, if Tony hasn't arrived yet, to go next door to the Pritchards' house and stay there."

I followed him into the homicide room, Dee Dee right on my heels. It was obvious that she was bursting with questions, but for now she kept her mouth shut.

Sergeant Hardison's explanation to Mom was brief but covered the important points. Mom told him that Tony wasn't there, and she promised to get out of the house immediately.

"She's worried about you," he told me. "She doesn't understand all that's happening, and she's frightened. I did my best to reassure her that you were perfectly safe."

169

Dee Dee gave him Eric's phone number, and he made the call, but there was no answer.

In Sergeant Hardison's car, on the way to our house, I filled him in. I told him everything. Dee Dee, in the backseat, made little squeaking, gasping noises as I related the entire story. She'd tell the neighborhood. She'd tell the whole world, but that no longer worried me.

"You talked to me about the DNA testing," I said to Sergeant Hardison. "If you could match Rosa's with the type A blood sample taken from the entry hall, wouldn't that be enough proof?"

"It should be strong proof, but we're still missing the murder weapon and the eyewitness."

"I think we can come up with an eyewitness," I answered. "Someone besides the Holts knew that Rosa was living there—Lupita, who lives next door in the Pritchard house."

"Lupita?" Dee Dee shrieked. "But she wouldn't know what happened to Rosa. Lupita said something about Rosa being deported, about Immigration."

I twisted around in the front seat to look at Dee Dee. "You told me she was so frightened, she was talking too fast for you to understand her. I think she was frightened for herself. She wants to be anonymous so that *she* won't be deported. Let's talk to Lupita and find out."

As we turned the corner into our street there was no sign of Tony's car. But, as Sergeant Hardison parked on the Pritchard driveway in the shade of the house, he called in for a unit to stake out our house.

Dee Dee rested her arms on the back of the front

170

seat and watched. "I've never been in a police car before," she said. "How do you make your calls?"

"It's a simple matter of pressing this switch." He demonstrated for Dee Dee's benefit, then said, "Come on. We'd better let Mrs. Darnell know that you're both all right."

Dee Dee was the first one out of the car, and she led us into her house.

Mom, who had Dinky in one arm, threw herself at me and held me so tightly, I could hardly breathe. Dinky protested loudly. "Sarah! Tell me what's going on!" Mom demanded.

"Tony is really Adam Holt," I explained, pulling away so I could talk. "Getting us together was a joke to Eric. That's all I think it was supposed to be—an 'in' joke I wouldn't understand but that he could secretly laugh about. Only it went much farther than I'm sure Eric had imagined."

"A joke!" Furious tears filled Mom's eyes.

Dee Dee walked in, leading Lupita by the hand. Lupita's eyes were huge, and she was trembling. "Immigration?" she whispered to Sergeant Hardison. Her knees wobbled, and she looked as though she were going to faint.

"No," he said. He took her arm, guided her to a chair in the Pritchard living room, and sat facing her. "Do you speak English?" he asked.

"*Un poco*—a little bit," she said, correcting herself.

"I am not going to have you deported," he said. "Understand?"

171

She nodded but continued to look wary.

Sergeant Hardison continued. "In fact, the district attorney's office will even keep you from being deported if you're needed as a witness."

Lupita was obviously a little confused with that sentence, so Dee Dee tried to translate. She finished by saying, "Sergeant Hardison is a police detective."

Lupita clutched the arms of the chair, her eyes wide with terror. "*¡Policía!* No!" she cried.

"Please, Lupita," Dee Dee said. "If you saw anything that happened at the Holts' house, tell us."

"Is all over," Lupita said, and pressed her lips together into a tight, thin line.

"She's still afraid," Mom murmured.

I knelt in front of Lupita and took her hands. "Rosa came to me," I told her. "She showed me herself. Then she showed me how she was stabbed to death. She even let me know where her body is hidden."

Lupita understood this. She gasped. "H-how could she do this?"

"In visions, in dreams," I told her.

Lupita jerked her hands from mine and shrank from me.

"I'm not evil," I said. "Rosa chose me so that I could help her. And she needs your help, too, so that she can rest."

Lupita began to cry and asked, "What does Rosa want me to do?"

"She only wants you to tell the truth. Please. Tell the detective what you know about Rosa and what you saw the day Rosa was killed."

172

Lupita pulled a tissue from her pocket and wiped her eyes. In a whispery, shuddery voice, fluctuating between English and Spanish, she told us that she knew Rosa. Sometimes, during the day, when the Pritchards and the Holts were at work and school, Lupita and Rosa would meet for a cup of tea or hot chocolate.

Adam Holt had frightened Rosa. Sometimes he'd acted very strange and had talked about evil things to her. Lupita ducked her head and said she couldn't repeat them. Rosa had wanted to leave the Holts, but she had no family, no one who knew or cared where she was; so there was nowhere for her to go.

"Do you know what happened to Rosa?" Sergeant Hardison asked.

"En la tarde—uh . . . afternoon, I go outside. I uh— sweep—" She got lost in a tangle of words, so Dee Dee helped. "To sweep the front porch?"

"Yes. But I did not sweep. I saw Adam Holt. I hid."

"What was Adam doing?" Sergeant Hardison asked.

"He drove pizza automobile away. I go in house. Later I looked out window and saw him walk back."

"Had you heard any sounds from the Holts' house?"

"No. *La* radio—" She stopped and fumbled for the next word.

Dee Dee interceded. "Lupita likes to play radio music while she's working. She likes it loud too."

"All right," Sergeant Hardison said to Lupita. "You were playing the radio and didn't hear anything." As she nodded vigorously he said, "Did you see Adam Holt go back into his own house?"

173

"*Sí.* But he came outside. *Con dos*—he bring two big bags from his house."

"Big bags? Trash bags?" Dee Dee asked.

Lupita nodded. "*Muy* heavy bags, hard for him to carry. One at a time." She made motions with her hands and said, "He put them in his automobile, in—uh—very back."

"She means the trunk," Dee Dee said.

"*Sí*—yes. Adam drive—" She finished the sentence with her hands, showing the direction.

"What time was this?" Sergeant Hardison asked.

"*Dos o dos y quarto.*"

"Did you know what was taking place?"

Dee Dee helped translate, and Lupita shook her head.

"But you knew later. What did you do when Adam Holt drove away?"

Lupita could barely speak. "I go to house. Look in window. I pound on door and ring doorbell, but Rosa *no es*—Rosa not come. I know Rosa was not there."

I couldn't help interrupting. "Lupita! When you learned about Darlene Garland's murder, you remembered the two bags. You knew that Rosa had been murdered, too, didn't you?"

Lupita fell back in the chair in an explosion of wails and tears. I caught the words *la policía,* but it was Dee Dee who finally was able to understand.

"She thinks she'll be in terrible trouble with the police because she didn't come forward with what she had seen. She thinks she'll be put in prison."

Sergeant Hardison reached forward and patted

174

Lupita's arm, smiling at her. "No one will harm you," he said. "You're a valuable witness. You're going to make our case solid by placing Adam Holt at the scene of the crime."

He made some calls and told us that an officer was already on the way to talk to Martin Holt, that every effort would be expended to pick up both Eric and Adam, and that the surveillance car was already in place on our block. Our house was being watched, and there had been no sign of Adam Holt in the vicinity.

"Could I ride back with you to get Mom's car?" I asked Sergeant Hardison. I didn't want to be there if Tony—Adam—came. I didn't want to see him arrested.

"Sure," Sergeant Hardison said. "I'll want to take an official statement from you, anyway."

"I'm going with you," Mom said. "I'm not going to let Sarah out of my sight!"

"You can't take Dinky," I told her, and took the cat from her arms. "I'll put her outside. She'll be all right."

"I'll need to take Lupita downtown for a statement too," Sergeant Hardison said, but Lupita burst into frightened tears again, and Mom and Dee Dee tried to calm her.

"I'll be with you!" Dee Dee shouted at Lupita, but Lupita was making so much noise, she couldn't hear her.

I couldn't stand it. "I'll wait for you in the car," I told them, but no one could hear me, either.

The moment I stepped outside, Dinky squirmed from my arms and was off like a streak, heading for our house. I didn't worry about her. She'd be all right. I walked over to the driveway and climbed into the passenger side of Sergeant Hardison's car, scrunching down so that I could lean my head back against the seat and try to relax.

Suddenly a hand gripped my shoulder, and a voice whispered from behind me, "Don't move, Sarah. Don't make a sound. I have a knife."

Chapter Fourteen

Tony!" I gasped for breath, and my heart began to hammer so loudly, I was sure he could hear it.

"I'm not going to kill you," he said. "I'm going to use you to help me get away from here."

I could tell from the direction of his voice that he was ducking low, behind the seat, so I knew he wouldn't be able to see what I was doing. With my fingertips I fumbled for the microphone and I felt for the switch. There! I flipped it on.

"Adam!" I said loudly. "There's nowhere we can go. Sergeant Hardison took the keys to his car with him."

"I know that," Adam said, and warned me by gripping my shoulder so hard that it hurt. "Keep your voice down!"

I wasn't sure how much of what we were saying could be picked up by the microphone. I wasn't even sure that what I said was being transmitted. I could only hope. "You told me you have a knife," I said. "What good

177

is it going to do? As soon as the sergeant comes out to his car, he'll find you here, and he has a gun."

Adam made a quiet, chuckling sound. "When you see him coming, you call out to him that I'm here, and you tell him to throw you his car keys. Then you'll drive away with his car. He won't use the gun. He couldn't take a chance on hitting you, and he won't know if I'll make good my threat with the knife."

In the rearview mirror I could see the two officers in the surveillance car heading cautiously, with guns drawn, toward the back of the sergeant's car. From the corner of my eye I caught a glimpse of Sergeant Hardison as he moved slowly across the Pritchards' front porch.

When Adam spoke again, his voice was so low and soft that I shivered, remembering its spell over me. "Sarah," he said, "don't try to think of a way out of this. Your 'spirits' can't help you now."

"I can help myself," I told him.

Maybe I sounded too confident. Something warned Adam. He rose behind me, just high enough to see the three policemen approaching. There was a flash of sunlight on metal as his knife appeared next to my face. I couldn't help flinching.

"That's it," he muttered. "Reach over slowly and roll down the window. Tell your sergeant to throw his keys inside the car."

"Give up, Adam," I said, "because I won't do it."

"If you don't, I'll kill you," he snapped.

"If I do drive away with you, it's a sure thing that you'll kill me. My chances are better here. Look at the police officers. Their guns are aimed at you. If you do kill

178

me here, you'll be caught immediately . . . or shot. And this time there'll be witnesses."

"Witnesses," he mumbled. I could almost hear him thinking.

Suddenly he made a quick movement, and I braced myself, trying not to scream, but the pressure was lifted from my shoulder, and the knife fell to the seat beside me. I twisted just in time to see Adam, his hands raised, before the police descended on the car.

I was jerked out in one direction, Adam in the other. I stood alone on the driveway, watching Tony—Adam—being led to the police car. His hands were cuffed behind his back, but his head was high, and there was even a slight smile on his face. I hated him for what he'd done, yet I remembered his kiss with a desire that shivered through my body.

"Why does he fascinate me?"

I wasn't aware that I'd said the words aloud until Sergeant Hardison, who had come up beside me, answered my question. "Evil is often fascinating."

"Why?" It came out like a sob.

"It has to be or it wouldn't exist."

"Sarah!" Mom came running from the Pritchard house, and I rushed to meet her. Right now I didn't want to think about Tony. Just like a little kid, I needed my mother.

■

They found Rosa's body in the clearing near the lake, just where I told them it would be. The murder weapon— the kitchen knife—was with her, and it matched the set that had belonged to the Holts.

"Rosa wants to be buried in consecrated ground," I told Mom and Dad. "Please, could we do this for her?"

Mom looked at me in near desperation. "Has she told you this? Has she appeared to you again?"

"No," I said. "It's just something I know she would want."

"We can do whatever you wish for Rosa," Dad reassured me. "The poor young woman. She had no one."

"She had me."

Mom patted my hand. "When you talk to Dr. Fulton—" she began, but I interrupted her.

"Cancel the appointment," I said. "It's over now, Mom. No more visits from the other world, no more visions. I feel sure of it. I don't need Dr. Fulton."

"But—" Mom began, then abruptly stopped. From the corner of my eye I had seen Dad touch her arm.

I walked to the window, held back the curtain, and watched the streetlights blink bright passages through the thickening dusk.

For just an instant, with a great wave of sorrow, a jumble of faces appeared in my mind—Rosa's, Tony's, Marcie's, Andy's. Faces from the past.

I took a deep breath. That's all they were—part of the past. And the past was where they'd stay.

But dwelling on the past wasn't for me.

I turned back to my parents, stepping into the brightness and warmth of the room, and smiled.

"See you later," I said. "I'm going to call Dee Dee."

About the Author

Joan Lowery Nixon is the author of more than seventy books for young readers, including *The Kidnapping of Christina Lattimore, The Séance,* and *The Other Side of Dark,* all winners of the Edgar Allan Poe Award, given by the Mystery Writers of America.

Ms. Nixon lives in Houston, Texas, with her husband.